THE CHAINS
THAT BIND US

THE CHAINS THAT BIND US

by

JASON CLENDENIN

Published in the United States
by eBooks2go, Inc.
1827 Walden Office Square, Suite 260, Schaumburg, IL 60173

ISBN-10: 1-5457-4720-2

ISBN-13: 978-1-5457-4720-9

Library of Congress Cataloging in Publication

THE CHAINS THAT BIND US

Volume 1

• • •

LOOK FOR THE SOUNDTRACK
The Chains That Bind Us
Including: Single "Trying So Hard to Survive"

JASON CLENDENIN

Contents

Foreword

The Chains That Bind Us. It is the legacy of slavery—the original sin. Laws were written, and a system was designed to subjugate people of color. It starts with the Middle Passage and slave ports. Enforced with laws, Whites Only signs, cross burnings, floggings, and lynchings. Empowered by political deception, societal condemnation, and religious betrayal. The numbers don't lie. Today it's clearly evident on our streets and in our courts. It's woven in the social and cultural fabric of our society. A mosaic of obstacles in housing, employment, and social and legal injustices. Mandates given to police and legislated policies that arrest men and women instead of providing them with opportunities, jobs, and education. It's in the number of unarmed men killed and in mass incarcerations. It's a system put in place to marginalize, deprive, and deny the progress of people of color. It is the fear and hatred of people of color and a desire by some to punish and ridicule them. It is the uneven hand of justice stacking courts and police forces that perpetuate this system. Young men and woman with few options, are convicted before adulthood. Condemned to prison system, poverty, or the morgue. We've gone from three-fifths of a vote to gerrymandering and other state-sponsored violations of basic civil liberties. It all starts with the dark legacy of slavery. Bodies violated, families destroyed, and faith tested. It's where behaviors were taught, and an entire people were oppressed. There were those who fought to help end slavery; then there were those who looked the other way as other benefited from slavery. Jim Crow laws were in effect until 1965, when the Civil Rights Act was ratified. The lingering effects of Jim Crow laws are evident today. We've gone from slavery and sharecropping to what I call a *concrete plantation*, where poverty is a commodity and a tool to control and exploit people of color. It all starts with slavery and the American plantation system, where people were sold, families were torn apart, and men and women were violated. These are the chains that leave lasting scars, both mental and physical. It is a system and legacy of fear and hatred that still plague our communities.

Numbers Do Not Lie
12 million enslaved; 2.4 million died in transport;
10.5 million arrived in the Americas.

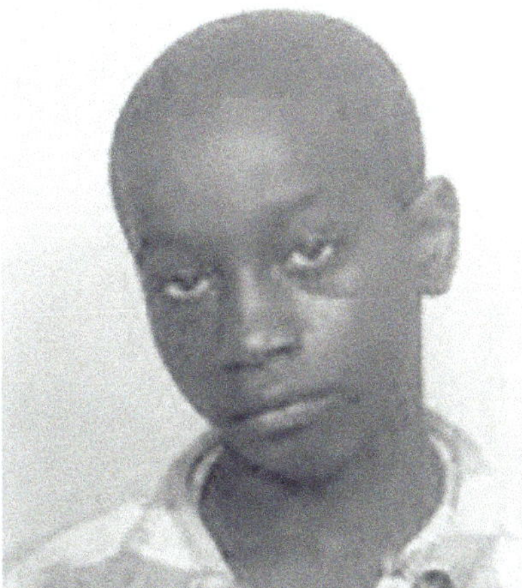

Dedicated to the **Young men**

THE KILLING OF YOUNG MEN OF COLOR

Lynching
Unarmed Shooting
Executed

EMMETT TILL, GEORGE STINNEY JR. TRAYVON MARTIN

Rest in Peace

SHORT STORY

PLANTATION

A SLAVE

NARRATIVE

PLANTATION STORY ABOUT SLAVE NARRATIVES

Overview

"PLANTATION" ADAPTED FROM A SCREEN PLAY

This collection is a walk through the history and the legacy of slavery, as told through a slave narrative, photographs, art, and poetry. The book is more of an artistic endeavor and will be released with an accompanying soundtrack. It is a little-known fact that 2019 is the four-hundred-year anniversary of slavery. The first slave arrived in the American colonies in 1619. This book uses prose, photos, art, and poetry to walk through the legacy of slavery. *Plantation*, adapted from a screenplay, explores slavery through the eyes of a former slave. In volume II, "Concrete Plantation," we will explore the lasting effects of slavery. Little is known about the period at the end of slavery and the years shortly after. Slaves would not know they were free for several years. Meanwhile, the atrocities of slavery lingered.

Roots was a groundbreaking book written by Alex Halley. It told the incredibly important story of slavery. Our book deals with one former slave's account of slavery as it came to an end. There are documented accounts from former slaves called the "Slave Narratives." These are government records detailing former slave's complaints, hardships, and the atrocities they endured. It is a historic documented account from the last living former slaves. Little was done with this information. The stories have never been told. Our story starts with the last days of the Civil War. For most of the plantations, the order of the day was business as usual. Slavery was still a major part of everyday life; change had not come yet to these areas. An investigator had recorded and documented a former slave's account of life on the Planation. The former slave, an older man at the time of the interview, reflects on his life on the plantation. He would eventually escape and become a solider in the Union army. This story is an account of his struggles.

CHAPTER
ONE

Chapter 1

Dedicated to Maria Martin & Juneteenth Day

June 19, 1865, Juneteenth, was marked to celebrate the belated announcement of the Emancipation Proclamation in 1865, nearly two years after slavery was officially ended in the United States. It became a day celebrated in forty-five states. My story is not an easy one to tell. I worked every day and was mercilessly whipped—hunted even though I was free. If I was caught, I was flogged to the bone. All this to pick cotton in the fields from sunup to sundown. That was my life—the brutality I've seen. I've seen women mercilessly beaten and robbed of their children, torn from their arms as they screamed in horror, never to see their child again. I watched as my family was sold into slavery, working for others who lived off the hard work men and women put in every day. Women watched as their husbands were beaten into submission; men watched as their wives' bodies were taken. That was my reality: not being able to protect my family from a horrible institution. President Lincoln said, "Slavery is founded in the selfishness of man's nature—opposition to it is in his love of justice." I felt that it was so much deeper than that. We lived every day at the sadistic pleasure of corrupt men who enjoyed putting us down. It made them feel superior. They tormented women and children because they could. Some who had not done anything but work hard were still beaten every day. It all started with the house. The plantation house, which slaves referred to as the big house, was beautiful, symmetrical, and white, sitting like a jewel in the center of a perfectly manicured landscape.

The long road leading to the big house was lined with trees. Stormy weather made the house look older from the moment the sunlight started fading to a blue darkness, gradually accented by lightning, thunder, and heavy rain. There was a huge field behind the house that stretched for miles, where thousands of slaves still picked cotton. Streams of lightning danced in the distance. As the wind whistled, I heard the faint sound of a child's voice singing, "I know someday we'll be free—freedom. Someday we'll be free. God is going to protect us. Someday we'll be free. He will watch over us. Someday we'll be free. Freedom, freedom, someday we will be free."

Footsteps pounding the ground and splashing the puddles cut the steady noise of the wind, the rain, and the child's singing. In the distance, several dogs barked wildly. Several men holding double-barreled shotguns approached the field, looking in all directions as thunder filled the air. A bad storm was growing worse. As the winds picked up speed, several slaves struggled against the elements, cringing at the flashes of lightning illuminating them every few minutes. Two overseers on horseback rode up to the field and stopped in front of each other, trying to steady their horses. Overseer Clayton, a young black man, swung his horse around. Overseer Hawkins, an imposing white man with a thick Southern drawl and roughly a decade older than Clayton, pulled his horse in closer.

"It's getting bad out here, boss," Clayton said, struggling to speak over the thunder. "Worse than I've seen in some time. Shouldn't we give them a break?"

"Let them work," Hawkins snarled back. Each breath is visible in the cold air. "They're slaves—it's all they're good for anyway." The slaves picked cotton under the watchful eyes of several other overseers, each with a shotgun in hand. The child's voice fell softer—one might detect an African accent. There are places God does not visit. Places where prayers are not answered, and his children are forgotten. When you cry, he doesn't hear you, but you can see his tears in the rain every day. These fields are unholy—countless had suffered and died here. The slaves called it their own hell—a grave for the living.

As Overseer Hawkins dismounted, he intensely scanned the area before marching past several slaves. He aggressively approached Jacob, a quiet young man, and stood inches away from his face.

"What do you think you're doing?" Hawkins barked, screaming over the thunder. "You're too slow. Move quicker. The longer it takes you to finish, the longer you stay out here!"

"My hands are freezing, boss," Jacob said.

"I don't care; get back to work," Hawkins answered, pushing Jacob to the ground as he walked away, laughing to himself. "Let's go! Keep working!" he yelled across the field. "If you folks don't work harder, you'll be out here all night!"

Off in the distance, Hawkins noticed a young woman struggling to keep up. Each piece of cotton she picked flew away in the wind. Dismounting his horse, who was getting more and more rattled by the thunder, he strutted over to her, smiling with sadistic delight when he realized who it is. "What do you think you're doing?" he asked.

"The best I can," Ellie responded, trying to speed up.

"Well, that's just not good enough. You were too good to even talk to me when you were in the big house," Hawkins said, smiling.

"No, I—"

"Shut up!" Hawkins yelled. "You were too good for me; then you got in trouble, and now you're in my house."

The rain poured down his face. He grabbed Ellie by the arm and pulled her off the ground.

"No, please, I can do better," Ellie cried. "Please, I can do better!"

"Shut up, or I'll kill you. I promise this will be your last day if you so much as make a sound." Hawkins threw her to the ground, tearing her dress and bruising her arm before violently snatching her up again.

A few yards away, Paul, another slave, slowly rose from his work as he watched the struggle escalate. He ran toward Hawkins and stood in his path.

"Get back to work!" Hawkins yelled.

"Listen to him, Paul. Please," Ellie begged.

"Leave her alone. She was doing the best she could," Paul said.

"What did you say to me?" Hawkins asked, amazed. "I said get back over there!"

While Paul stood his ground, he didn't notice two other well-built overseers lurking behind him. One of them kicked him in the back, knocking him to the ground. As he struggled to break free, one of the men wrapped a rope around his neck while Hawkins continued pulling Ellie in the direction of an outhouse.

"No! Get off me!" Paul screamed, choking.

Overseer Hawkins pulled Ellie toward a makeshift outhouse. As she struggled to fight him off, another overseer entered with a double-barreled shotgun and stood watch. Several slaves looked on as Paul was being choked to death. Saddened, they looked away. A child slave began to pray.

Finally reaching the outhouse, Hawkins pulled Ellie behind it. Violently tearing at her clothing with one hand, he took off his belt with the other.

"You still think you're better than me?" he screamed. "Master Sneely put you in the field, and now you are mine. You are my property."

"Please, no," Ellie yelled, loudly sobbing. "Oh Lord!"

A bird circled the outhouse before rising higher into the stormy sky. It must have heard Ellie's clothing rip and her muffled crying over the sound of the child's voice praying.

"God, please, why don't you listen? Fly away—I wish I could fly away. Sometimes I wish I could fly away from this place," the child prayed.

Ellie prayed, too, as she cried, "Lord, please—"

"Shut up!" Hawkins yelled. "Don't you know? God don't hear you out here in these fields."

"Why? Why, God?" Ellie screamed. "What did I do?"

"You were born," Hawkins answered.

CHAPTER
TWO

NEGROES
FOR SALE.

Will be sold at public auction, at Spring Hill, in the County of Hempstead, on a credit of twelve months, on Friday the 28th day of this present month, 15 young and valuable Slaves, consisting of 9 superior Men & Boys, between 12 and 27 years of age, one woman about 43 years who is a good washer and cook, one woman about twenty-seven, and one very likely young woman with three children.

Also at the same time, and on the same terms, three Mules, about forty head of Cattle, plantation tools, one waggon, and a first rate Gin stand, manufactured by Pratt &Co.

Bond with two or more approved securities will be required. Sale to commence at 10 o'clock.

E. E. Hundley,
W. Robinson,
H. M. Robinson.

Chapter 2

Dedicated to Harriet A. Jacobs and the Underground Railroad

Baton Rouge, Louisiana, 1937
Seventy-Four Years after Slavery Ended

On one of the hottest days Baton Rouge had seen in decades, George Langley drove his 1935 Ford up a long, winding, bumpy dirt road. At thirty-five years old, he'd become known as one of the government's more idealistic federal investigators. Driving with one hand on the wheel, he took off his hat, wiped his forehead, and glanced at a folder on the seat next to him. Upon a second glance, he opened it and scanned a stack of letters. Fumbling through the pile, he spotted a memo with a directive reading: "Document a claim from a former slave, Mr. John."

"They act like this is easy to do," Langley muttered, "when all the slaves have been free for over fifty years." Langley had been traveling for some time, and he was tired and irritable. "I can't believe they want me to find him and document his claim. It would be nice if they put up a signpost reading 'Former Slaves Live Here,'" he said, shaking his head, desperate for sleep.

When he reached the end of the road, he noticed the remains of a burned-down house, and he got out of the car for further inspection. "This must have been some big house." Langley marveled at the wreckage, taking off his hat and rubbing his head. A river flowed through the rest of the plantation's lush, hilly landscape. The sunlight shimmered off the water. Birds sang and flew overhead.

Preoccupied with the remains, Langley didn't notice a shadow creeping over his shoulder. A man holding a shotgun quickly knocked Langley to the ground. His glasses flew off his face. Looking up, he couldn't make out the figure standing over him, blocking the sun. As he grabbed his glasses and put them back on, he tried to stand up. He saw an elderly but robust black man holding a shotgun. He knocked Langley to the ground again, pointing the gun at his head.

"What business do you have here?" the old man snarled.

Langley nervously reached for his badge, but after giving it a second thought, he put both hands in the air, surrendering. "My name is George—George Langley. I am a federal investigator sent here to document claims made by former slaves."

"Document? For what?"

"You sent us letters," Langley continued.

"Letters?" John asked. After thinking for a moment, John replied, "That was over fifty years ago. What? They got lost in the mail?"

"It took some time to find you," Langley said.

"Why?" John asked, suddenly becoming angrier. "I haven't gone anywhere. And you don't look like no federal investigator."

"And you don't speak like someone who's been a slave," Langley said, smiling. "I have my badge in my shirt. I'm just going to reach for it. Don't shoot me."

"Go ahead, but slowly. You don't want your head blown off, and, frankly, I don't want to blow it off for you."

Langley reached in his shirt and pulled out his badge. "Here, see? I also have one of your letters you can check."

"Well, it's about time someone paid attention to my letters," John said, helping Langley to his feet. Fixing his suspenders, he reached out and shook Langley's hand. They exchanged a smile.

"You speak very well," Langley said again.

"Comes from working in the big house. Miss Celia wanted us to be able to write, read, and speak like she did."

The two of them walked over toward the house.

"I've been driving for a week, trying to track you down," Langley said.

"Well, you found me."

"Is there some place I can get cleaned up?" Langley asked.

"You sure you ain't with those fools? You know, who wear sheets over their heads?" John countered, shaking his head, serious. "Because I can't have that in my house."

"Trust me—I'm not."

John stared him down as he wiped his forehead. "It can get a hundred degrees out here sometimes. Why don't you come with me over to the shade?"

"I'm getting too old for this," Langley muttered to himself.

They walked into John's intimate two-room house. Everything was neatly organized, and the walls were lined with pictures. The front door was open, with a closed mesh-wire screen door to keep the flies out. Langley saw John sitting outside on the porch, his back to the door. He took the opportunity to look around inside. There were old pictures and personal mementos everywhere.

"No one is this neat," Langley murmured.

John sat in a rocking chair, slowly rocking with a pipe in his hand, aimlessly staring out into the field. "Yes, our prayers have been answered," he spoke into the air. "I will tell him our stories. Hopefully it will put you to rest." He paused, as if listening to someone. "I know, I know—he doesn't look like no fancy, know-it-all federal investigator to me either."

Back inside, Langley discovered military medals on John's dresser, alongside an old American flag. "He must have fought in the war." Langley looked through the screen door and walked toward it when he heard John talking to someone. Looking around, he didn't see anyone. "Who were you talking to?"

"You wouldn't believe me if I told you."

"You don't have much in your house, but I tell you, you have to be the cleanest person I've ever met," Langley said, immediately giving up.

"This house is all I need. Most slaves were like that—clean. There are a lot of lies about us."

"And I've heard a lot of them."

"I want the truth to be heard today, like the fact that we fought for this country. And proudly, I might add."

"Yes, I saw the medals in your house." Langley curiously pressed on, growing excited.

John smiled. "Oh really? Instead of Mister Langley, we should call you Mister Nosy."

"Sorry, I—"

"During the war we fought hard and helped build this country. Right now we are free, but we still don't have the same rights as everyone else."

"Hopefully that will change soon. Do you live here by yourself?"

"No, my friends come and visit me from time to time," John answered.

Langley looked around, puzzled. "Friends?"

"You probably won't be able to see them, but they are here. They won't leave."

"Who?"

John leaned forward. "Do you believe in God?"

"No."

"By the end of this story, you will."

"I don't understand."

"The souls of the folks who lived and died here—they are still here."

Smiling, Langley looked around the air, almost mockingly. "The souls of the people who lived here?"

"Yes, I know how it sounds."

"It sounds crazy—you mean it *is* crazy."

"I can hear their voices in the wind, see their faces in the rain, feel their pain in the waters. 'Testaments of water,' my uncle used to say."

"Testaments of water—what's that?"

"With water comes a baptism, a spiritual rebirth. When something tragic happens, there is a need for truth and justice, which is a form of rebirth. So their voices have got to be heard. It's like an open wound. Until it's properly healed, the wound just lingers, infecting everything around it."

Langley wasn't expecting this, but he wanted to connect with John. "That's why I'm here—to record your experiences. I brought a tape recorder with me." He pulled it out and pressed record. "I am George Langley, federal investigator, here to investigate and record the testaments of a former slave, a one John—I mean, Mister John—for the United States government." He spoke loudly into the recorder, looking up to smile at John from time to time.

"Turn it off," John said, shaking his head.

"Why?"

"Turn it off," John said louder and more sternly. He reached over and stopped the recording himself.

"Why did you do that?"

"I'm going to tell you the story. You tell the world."

"I know," Langley said, "And I have to record it."

John held up a pencil. "This is all you need—it's like magic wand. I waved it sixty years ago. It was all I needed to get you out here."

"Listen, we have procedures, and this—"

John abruptly cut him off. "I will say some things on the tape. I'll make it sound good for you, but for now, if you want my story, no tape. I don't like those things."

Langley looked at John for a while and gradually flashed a half-smile. Reluctantly, he took the pencil and began writing.

"Have you ever been in love?" John asked, leaning forward. He repeated the question in a soft, endearing tone. "Really in love?"

"Excuse me?"

"Have you ever been in love?"

"I have a wife and two kids."

"Well, hold them tight, and don't them go. I was once fortunate enough to have found love."

"What does this have to do with your claim?"

John pointed to Langley's notepad. "How about less talking and more writing?"

CHAPTER THREE

Chapter 3

Dedicated to Mary Prince and the Slave Narratives

Ten Years before the End of Slavery

John ran through a narrow path in a cotton field, watching the older slaves work. An eternally optimistic twelve-year-old, he ran through the tall yellow-gray corn husks as if he were in a beautiful field of flowers and green grass on a sunny day. His whole life was filled with stories—stories that took him far from these fields and to other places. Places where he was free. His mother would talk about folks living free and peacefully up North. John told her that one day he would take her there.

It was hard not to notice the walls around them, but she tried to shelter him as best as she could. John ran toward Overseer Russell, one of the black overseers, who sneered down at John from the top of his horse.

"You better slow down, boy," Overseer Russell said.

"Yes, Mister Russell."

"Where are you going?"

"Back to the house."

"Well, go ahead, be on your way. Wouldn't want you to get in any trouble."

"Yes sir. Good day." Once out of Russell's sight line, John continued to run the length of the property, taking in everything and everyone he passed. John and his mother were different because they worked in the big house. It was difficult, brutal labor for the slaves who worked in the field. John had been born to a black mother and a white father. It was a mark he would carry with him for the rest of his life. His mother had given him the name John. She had always heard folks call each other "mister," so she called her son Mr. John.

The biggest injustice of slavery was stripping slaves of their last names—their heritage.

John burst into the kitchen and saw his mother, Marlene, seated in a rocking chair, sewing a shirt, singing her favorite hymn: "We will be just fine, putting my faith in the sunshine. Putting my faith in the Lord."

She stopped singing and brightened up when she saw him. "Now, Mister John, you know you are not supposed to be running in the house," she scolded.

"Sorry, Mom, but I have something for you." He opened his hand to reveal a flower. Marlene was taken aback, delighted.

"I forgive you this time," she said, smiling. "It is beautiful. Where did you get it?"

"From behind the house."

"I told you not to go there, and you promised me," she said, her tone changing. "Now I'm not telling you again. Stop going over there."

"OK, I won't," John said, crossing his fingers as his mother hugged him tightly. He couldn't understand why she didn't want him going there, so he kept going anyway.

CHAPTER
FOUR

Chapter 4

Dedicated to Old Elizabeth and the Thirteenth Amendment

Cathryn Kelly, Celia Gray, and Jane Corey were seated in a circle, dressed in their Sunday best, sipping tea. Marlene briskly walked in with a tray, and Miss Cathryn nodded at her as she set another fresh pot on the table.

Marlene worked for Miss Celia. She didn't like slaves and was hard on her. Miss Celia ran a group who would organize a big Southern ball. Every year the lady's group would get together to discuss the ball. It was mainly an excuse to gossip.

"I can't wait till the ball. I've already picked out a dress," Celia said in her heavy aristocratic Southern accent. The only people she loathed more than slaves were abolitionists.

"Times sure are changing," Cathryn added. "Have you heard? They are talking about freeing the slaves."

"Can you imagine?" Celia replied, cringing." Rest assured, they will never be free."

"But we can't keep them like this forever," Cathryn insisted.

"I just don't know what we will do if they free them," said Jane, the youngest in the group, in almost a whisper. "We can't afford to hire help."

"Since the North doesn't need slaves anymore, now they have a conscience?" Celia said. "It won't happen."

"Remember, they're people, and people shouldn't be mistreated," Cathryn said. "They deserve their freedom."

"So what are we supposed to do, then?" Jane nervously asked. "If we have to pay them, we wouldn't make any money. My husband says without slaves, there is no South."

"We can't be blinded by money," Cathryn replied. "They are people like you and me, and they are suffering."

As Celia patiently listened, she grew more put off by the minute. "My dear, talk like that could get you killed in these parts. If you like them so much," she added, breaking an uncomfortable silence, "you should move up North and be with them."

"She didn't mean—" Jane cut in.

"I know what she meant," Celia snapped. "And, might I add, for the record, they are not human like us. Why do you think they make them three-fifths of a human?"

"That's just so their vote doesn't count," Cathryn fired back.

"They're human—I've seen them laugh and cry," Jane squeaked out.

"I've even had to watch one die trying to escape. Just to be free," Cathryn said, shaking her head.

"No," said Celia, shaking her head in a different way. "They are nothing like us. God put them here to serve us—same as cattle. That's their place."

"I just don't know," Cathryn said. "You read the Bible. What's happening to those people is a sin."

Celia leaned forward, now completely vexed. "Where—where does it say slavery is a crime?" she said as calmly as possible. "Show me the passage. You can't, because it isn't in the Bible. All this talk about freeing the slaves—what would they do if they weren't slaves? You look at Marlene," she continued, "she's a good one who learned how to read, write, and speak proper like us. But she's still a slave and will always be one." She signaled for Marlene to come over. "She has been with us since she was a teen," she continued as Marlene walked over. "What would happen to her if she weren't here? I suppose some men would have their way with her. It's not like she's smart enough to do anything. Marlene, you are happy here, aren't you?"

"Yes, Miss Celia."

"All this talk about freeing the slaves. You prefer being a slave, don't you?"

Marlene stared at her for a second before Cathryn nervously chimed in.

"I don't think anyone wants to be a slave, Celia."

Celia ignored her and stared at Marlene.

"Don't you?" Celia asked, raising her tone.

"Yes, Miss Celia."

"See? Just like I told you. They love it. I mean, what else would they do?"

Marlene gave Celia a smile. Suddenly, Carl, Celia's youngest son, ran into the room and headed toward Marlene, giving her a hug, passing up his mother.

"Aunt Marlene!" he squeals, flashing an explosively bright smile. Marlene smiled back and bent down to hug him. Sensing Miss Celia's displeasure, she stood up and pulled back.

"We went down to the creek and picked up worms," Carl said.

"Carl, stop calling her your aunt, and come give your mother a hug," Celia coldly said, unable to mask her envy.

Carl didn't respond.

"Carl," she said again, raising her voice.

Carl walked over to his mother and unenthusiastically hugged her. "Sorry, Mom."

"You would think she was their mother," Celia told her friends as Martin, her eldest son, strolled into the room, nodding toward Marlene before walking to his mother.

"Mom, the slaves don't have food," Carl said with noticeable concern. "Can I bring them some after dinner?"

"You will do no such thing," Martin interjected. "They have all they need."

"No, they don't. Why do they have to live like that?"

"It's the way it's always been, and the way it will always be," Martin said as his mother approvingly looked on.

"One day it's going to change," Carl said.

"Young man, stop talking like that right now!" Celia said with surprise. "They are that way because that's the way God intended it!"

"But they—"

Celia slapped him. "Don't talk back to me."

Everyone stared at Carl with embarrassment, including his mother. Carl ran out of the room.

"I don't agree with him," Martin said, "But you didn't have to hit him."

His mother turned around and took a sip of tea, trying to contain her anger. "You can go with him, Martin."

"Now you got us both in trouble," Martin muttered to Marlene on his way out.

A cloud of tension fell over the quiet room as Celia glowered at Marlene. When Marlene finally turned to leave, her head lowered, and she clenched her teeth. In the hallway, she saw Carl crying, his back against the wall.

"Don't cry," she whispered.

"Why does she have to be so mean?"
"She just has a different way—that's all."

"She yells at everyone."

As Carl sobbed, Marlene hugged him tightly, trying to console him. Farther down the hallway, Martin looked on. He and Marlene briefly made eye contact before Martin abruptly turned and walked in the other direction.

"You're a big boy, so let me see that smile," Marlene said to Carl, tickling him. "Why don't you go downstairs? I may have something sweet for you in the kitchen."

Carl brightened and ran toward the staircase. Marlene slowly followed, aimlessly looking ahead as she moved forward.

CHAPTER FIVE

Chapter 5

Dedicated to Mattie J. Jackson—Abolitionist

Later that afternoon, John sneaked over to the other side of the plantation—an area reserved for the sick, elderly, and injured. It was an area where slaves were left to die. He walked down a small dirt road through leaves and rough tree branches. A small gust of wind occasionally blew some leaves around John's feet. There was no grass, and the closer he got, the more abandoned this part of the property appeared. He entered past a small iron-rod gate; the area resembled a small village. Five old mud houses and a wooden shack sat in a circle. Several slaves lied motionless on the ground against the walls of the mud houses. There were both males and females, and every age demographic was represented. John studied them in awe; they couldn't do much more than gaze back in despair. This place was unlike anything he had ever seen before, and it was just outside the property.

It was hard to tell the living from the dead. Flies flew around their faces and landed on their bodies.

It was as if John had walked into hell. The looks on their faces still haunted him to this day.

John looked around and realized he shouldn't have walked to that side of the plantation. As he quietly turned to leave, he noticed a man hanging from a rope overhead. Frightened, he ran into a heavy brush. He knelt and prayed.

"Yea, though I walk through the valley of the shadow of death, I will fear no evil. God protect me. I don't understand—what did they do wrong?" John stuttered. He was panicked and out of breath. "Please, God, answer me."

But no one replied. His mom used to say, "When God is ready, he will answer." But John had to take the first step in order for God to do the rest.

An old woman—hunched over, wrapped in a blanket, dressed in rags—walked behind him as he finished his prayers. John turned to look at her, and she removed the shawl covering her face. One of her eyes was missing, and there was a scar on her face. She didn't say anything; she just watched his expression.

John screamed and ran behind a tree a little farther away. "Please don't kill me," he yelled, panting. When John peered out from behind the tree, he saw the woman on the ground, crying. He walked over to her. "Don't cry."

"You would, too, if every time you showed your face children ran from you, screaming."

"I didn't mean you no harm."

"What are you doing here? Speak up—you're not supposed to be here."

"Are you a witch?"

"You come to my home, asking if I'm a witch? I wish I was so I could strike you down."

"I'm not afraid of you," John said with his head held up high, unsure of where this new confidence came from.

"You're a brave boy. Brave boys grow up to do big things. What brings you here?"

"I just wanted to know—"

"What happens here?" she answered, finishing his sentence.

They both looked around the little village, gazing at the sickly people congregating outside of the shacks. "When they feel we can't work in the field or in the house no more, this is where we're sent," the old woman explained.

"Why don't they help you?"

"Child," she quickly responded, laughing, "we are slaves. They don't care about us. We work for them, and when they finish with us, they throw us out like garbage. They want a strong back or a firm backside. In my day, I was pretty. I used to work in the house. I had a bad master. He would pull me out of house and beat me. No reason—just to punish me. His sons—all of them evil. One day I said no more," she pointed to her missing eye, "and this is what I got."

"One day I am going help all the slaves," John announced, still hanging on to his newfound confidence.

The old woman laughed again. "You? What can you do?"

"I can help."

"It has been like this for years. I don't think it's ever going to change. You should be getting home. You are a good boy."

John reached out his hand to help her up. To her surprise, it was was the first time anyone had spoken to her with kindness.

"You speak very good—and such good manners," she said.

"Miss Celia makes us learn to speak good. I mean well—speak well. I can read too."

"Can you?" she asked, unable to hide her excitement. "I was never allowed to read, but I've carried around a letter Master gave me before he sent me here. Can you read it to me?"

"OK," John said. He reached for the bag she pointed to and placed it in her hand.

"This bag is all I have in the world," she said, opening it to take out two pieces of paper tied in string. She carefully handed the papers to John, who untied the string and read the first letter. He placed his finger on the paper, sounding out the words "F-r-e-e—"

"I thought you said you can read. I can't read, but I'm better than that, and I only got one eye."

"This one says you are free," John reported.

"I know that one. But what good is free if you can't live? Read the other one—read the other one."

"I'm not that good."

"Please, try."

"Ethel—" he sounded out.

"Ethel—that's my name!"

"Ethel, made it up North. Will send for you—Love, Paul."

"He made it?" she asked, crying, happily surprised. She lied down on the ground, looking up at the sky.

"I have to go now," John said, getting more uncomfortable.

"He made it. I can't believe it," the old woman kept saying to herself, smiling, not noticing that John had walked off into the woods on his way home.

When he came back to visit her a week later, she had died. She died alone, but folks say she went with a smile.

CHAPTER
SIX

Chapter 6

Dedicated to Jared Maurice Arter and Nat Turner's Revolt

Martin entered the kitchen and watched Marlene cutting vegetables. "Why are you trying to steal my brother?" he asked, coming closer. "Because of you, Momma took to his face."

"I treat him no different than I treat you."

"No, you treat him nice."

"Martin, you know I care for you and your brother and always will."

"No, you're just like the rest. When Momma gets tired of you, they kick you out the house and into the field."

"If that's what your mother wants, I will go. That doesn't take away from the fact that I treated both of you as if you were my own."

"Don't say that—don't even think it. You don't understand—we had another housekeeper."

"Yes, before me." Marlene seemed puzzled.

"My first word as a child to her was 'Mommy.'"

"These things happen."

"I couldn't stop saying it, and my mother hated it. Every time I called her 'Mommy,' she got whipped. Until they put her out in the field, where she died. All because I called her 'Mommy.'"

"That's not your fault."

"I know it's not," Martin shot back. "I just don't want my brother to go through what I did."

"I understand. Thank you, Master Martin."

Martin looked at her sadly.

****

That night, seated outside a large window of the big house, John patiently waited for his mother to open it. Marlene came to the window, smiling at him. John's face lit up as he heard the music wafting out from inside.

Miss Celia would listen to music every night. She used to open the window so John and Marlene could listen to it.

The music abruptly stopped. "Marlene, come into the room now!" Celia yelled.

In the distance, John often heard music from the slaves. As bad as life could get, there was always magic—all around. "Someday we will be free. Freedom, someday we will be free," John heard the slaves singing from the field, the beat steadily swelling. "Someday we will be free. Freedom, someday we will be free."

****

The next day John ran through the field to a small pond where his Uncle Joe tried to catch fish. Gentle, but built like an ox, Joe threw his hat down in frustration.

"Lord, now we know I don't catch any fish, I catch a beating," Joe said to God. "So, if you can help me out a little, I'd be much obliged."

John walked over to him. "Uncle Joe?"

Joe smiled with delight. "John, good day to you."

"Good day to you. Have you caught any fish?" he asked, sitting down.

"I'm just getting started."

Uncle Joe had served in the war, for the Confederate army, and became a hero. If a master didn't want to go, he could send a slave in his place.

"Tell me again how you saved all those white folks in the battle."

"Sure. We had come to this lake. All the soldiers were scared to cross it, so they made me go. I get to the other side, and I see there is an ambush waiting for us. I go running and calling to them to run. They get out of there just before they could trap us."

A small group of Confederate soldiers moved in toward an embankment. Soldiers, led by a captain dressed in an army uniform, rode toward a ravine on horseback. They looked around and couldn't see over a hill. They signaled for a group of black soldiers to go ahead of them. Uncle Joe was at the front and slowly made his way to the other side. Once there, he saw the large force waiting to ambush them.

John looked on, shaking his head. "Wow!"

"I got a letter sent from the captain to Master for saving them from the ambush."

John looked back at the fishing line. "Still no fish?"

Joe waved his hand. "Not yet, but with a little bit of magic …"

"Momma says there's no such thing as magic."

"Yes, there is. We are alive, aren't we? As hard as it is to survive, we are still here. Just as clear as you are standing there. Matter of fact, this lake has magic."

"Really?"

"Sometimes I just put my hands over the water, and it tells me things—testifies." He placed his hand out over the water. "You just place your hands out over the water and believe we are going to get fish, and we will."

"Momma says that's what makes no sense."

"Yes, it does. Water gives life—it's everywhere. When it rains, God weeps for us. When a pastor dips us in the water to baptize us, it's to give us new life. If you believe, anything is possible."

"Do you think we will be free?"

"That's what the armies is fighting over—us being free. It can happen. Here, put your hands out over the water and believe we can get a fish. Close your eyes."

John closed his eyes tightly, held his hands out over the water, and made a wish. Joe opened one eye to look up at the sky, gesturing like he was talking to God.

"For the kid," Joe said under his breath.

John concentrated hard, but nothing happened. "I don't think it's working."

"Let me try."

The fishing rod moved, and the string started to pull. Joe ran over and reeled in the fish.

"It's working! It's working!" John squealed.

"Well, I'll be … I can't believe it," Joe said to himself, smiling. "I mean, I said it would, didn't I?"

Joe handed John the fish by the string, and John took off running and screaming with it. This was the part he had always hated. They wanted the fish to be fresh, so he had to move fast, but having the fish's scales so close to his own skin made him squeamish.

"Thank you," Joe said, laughing, looking up. "I owe you."

CHAPTER
SEVEN

Chapter 7

Dedicated to Lewis Charlton and the *Liberator*

Marlene walked into Celia's bedroom to straighten up. She carefully fixed the bed and arranged each perfume bottle on the dresser. She looked at herself in the mirror and picked up one of the perfumes to smell it. Suddenly, Celia entered the room.

"What do you think you're doing?" she yelled in a choppy, condescending tone.

"Nothing, I was just—"

"You were just what? Stealing from me? That's what you were doing!"

"No, I was just smelling."

Celia stormed over to Marlene and slapped her across the face. Marlene looked up at her.

"Don't you dare look me in the eye," Celia said, even more incensed than before. "Your job is to tend to the house and your duties. I don't want to see you up here touching anything. Is that understood?"

"Yes, Miss Celia."

"When I talk to you and ask you a question, you make sure you answer me. Do you hear me?"

"Yes, miss."

"Now go on about your chores. Make sure everything is done. We have the ball coming up. Everything thing must be in order."

"I will see to it, miss."

"You can go."

Marlene walked out of the room and closed the door behind her, trying to fight back tears. Coming in from outside, John saw her leaving the room and ran over.

"John, what are you doing in the house?"

"Mom, we catch a fish—me and Uncle Joe."

"You 'caught' a fish," Marlene corrected him.

"Sorry, we caught a fish."

"How many times do I have to tell you—Uncle Joe is going to get you in trouble, with his stories. Stay away from him."

"He is my friend."

John noticed his mother holding the side of her face. "Are you all right?"

"I just got something in my eye," Marlene said, teary-eyed. "Now come with me downstairs."

John knew she wasn't all right. She couldn't hide things from him as successfully as she had assumed. Her pain was John's pain.

***

A few hours later, Marlene held John in her lap, in her sleeping quarters, which was a small, well-kept room next to the kitchen. Celia's husband, Michael, opened the door and peeked in, motioning for Marlene to come out. Marlene carefully, reluctantly laid John on the bed, placing a sheet over him before walking out and closing the door behind her. Marlene and Michael walked further downstairs into the basement. Michael walked over to a lamp and turned the light on so he could see Marlene more clearly.

"I wish it were another time, where we could be together," he said.

"I can't wait for the day when I can be free. You promised that John and I would be freed."

"In time, you may get your wish. The North is looking to outlaw slavery."

"You promised me that you'd free us."

"In time. I haven't been able to yet, but soon." He walked over to Marlene, slowly untying her dress. When she struggled to stop him, he violently shook her.

"Why do you treat me like this?" he asked softly.

"You promised."

"Give me more time. Do you think he knows?"

"Knows what?"

"Your boy—that I am his father?"

"No, I told him his daddy ran off long ago."

"If it ever were to get out, I'd be ruined. We have to see to it that it remains a secret."

"Just like you and me."

As Michael continued to unfasten her clothing, she looked away with a sad, hurt look.

CHAPTER

EIGHT

Chapter 8

Dedicated to Lucinda Davis and Stations/Safe Houses

One bright, sunny day, John ran out of the back of the big house, when he heard the noises. A horse-drawn wagon filled with slaves slowly made its way onto the property. Every so often, new slaves would come in, and John always hoped his dad would be one of them. As he ran and chased after the wagon, he hoped his father would call his name. Marlene had told him it was hard on men to see their children as slaves and their wives abused and mistreated. Some couldn't deal with the pain, so they just up and left. Better to be alone and in pain than watch those they love die a slow death.

Just as John began to give up hope on these latest arrivals, he noticed a young lady and struggled to get a better look. As the wagon came to a stop, he saw her staring back at him. Her smile stopped him in his tracks.

That was the first time he saw her. She looked like an angel; she was the most beautiful thing he had ever seen.

John ran around the property—through a wooded area and through the back door of the house, after several attempts trying to get it open. In the kitchen, two slaves were snapping and cutting green beans at a table. He rushed over to his mom, sewing in the corner.

"Mom, there is this girl, and she is here!"

"Slow down. What girl?"

"I have just seen an angel."

"Tell me about her," Marlene said, smiling, still sewing.

"She was in the wagon, and she's the prettiest thing I have ever seen. She looks like a doll."

"Really? I thought you said you didn't like girls."

"You have to see this one," he said, giving his mom a big hug.

Marlene hadn't seen John so excited before. She was concerned for the girl, as she knew how difficult it was in the field. Their masters were bad, but the overseers were cruel. If she were in the field, she wouldn't survive. John never knew that his mother spoke to Miss Celia to arrange for the girl to be in the house.

When Marlene entered the parlor with a tray of tea, Celia sat by the window, looking outside. Marlene placed the tray down, poured a cup, and carefully brought it over. Celia accepted it without saying a word. After Marlene walked back over to collect the tray, she paused for a second, mustered more courage than she thought she had, and walked back to Celia.

"That's all, Marlene," Celia said when she saw Marlene approach her a second time.

"I beg your pardon—can I ask you a question? It's about the kitchen."

"Be quick with it. I have friends coming over."

"Well, we have three girls in the kitchen," Marlene said nervously. "I was just thinking—"

"Out with it," Celia cut her off.

"I was thinking we sure could use a little extra help."

"You already have three girls. Why do you need another?" Celia asked. "Someone else to sleep with my husband?" she added after a long pause.

Silence fell over the room. Celia rose to her feet.

"Miss, I—" Celia's intensity silenced her.

"What? Do you think I'm stupid, Marlene?"

"I have never … I—"

"I know you have no choice. It's not like you can say no."

"I'm sorry, Miss Celia."

"You think I want to hear you're sorry?" Celia snapped, clenching her teeth and fists. "If you breathe this to a soul, so help me, you will die in them fields. I couldn't imagine what people would say if they found out."

"Yes, Miss Celia."

"We just got a new load of slaves. They are in the barn. Choose the one you want. Make sure you clean her up before you bring her in my house."

"Yes, Miss Celia."

"You can leave now," Celia instructed, returning to her chair and cup of tea.

Marlene picked up the tray and struggled to hold back tears as she walked out, closing the door behind her and proceeding down the hall. Overcome with emotion, she stepped into a side room and closed the door behind her. She slid down the wall and fell to the floor, crying uncontrollably. Clutching herself with both arms, she tightly held herself in fetal position.

Marlene had always made sacrifices for her son. God only knows some of things she had to do, but somehow she managed to hold on to her dignity.

Later that day, the barns was filled with slaves as Marlene entered dressed in a clean maid's uniform, holding John's hand. When he saw the girl they were looking for, he abruptly let go of Marlene, wanting to come off as more mature. His mother saw who he was looking at and walked toward her. "She is pretty," she whispered to John.

"Mom," John said, embarrassed. They walked over to Ellie, who was seated on the floor, wearing a tattered old dress. She straightened up as she saw Marlene come closer.

"Hi, my name is Marlene."

"Yes, Miss, I'm Ellie."

"What's your last name?"

"I don't know," Ellie said.

"That's fine," Marlene said, smiling. "Ellie's a pretty name. I work in the kitchen. Would you like to work in the house?"

As soon as Marlene returned to the kitchen with Ellie and John behind her, she showed Ellie around, pointing things out to her. As she did so, Ellie looked back at John, who was a couple of paces behind them. Finally fed up with John's silent staring and smiling, Ellie marched over to him and spoke to him for the first time—words he would never forget: "What are you smiling at?"

That night Marlene walked through the house, making sure all the doors were closed and the windows were locked. She pulled at the knobs as she passed each door. Passing Carl's room, she opened the door to check on him. He was only half asleep and woke up when he saw the door open. "Marlene?" he whispered.

Marlene entered the room and closed the door behind her. "Yes, Master Carl."

"I can't sleep," he said, sitting up. "I keep having bad dreams."

"That's all right," she said reassuringly. "When I have bad dreams, I just think of good times, and those bad dreams just go away."

"How is it being a slave?"

"Uh, it's hard," Marlene said, taken aback. "But we manage."

"One day I am going to free you."

"How are you going to do that?" Marlene asked, smiling.

"I haven't figured that part out," Carl said after giving it some quick thought. "But one day I will."

"Hush now."

"You have always been like a mother to me."

"You get some rest now."

Carl reached out his arms and embraced Marlene. She hugged him back and laid him down on the bed. Pulling the blanket up over Carl's shoulders, she tucked him in.

CHAPTER NINE

Chapter 9

Dedicated to Moses Grandy and American Civil War Soldiers

Like every year, Celia was filled with excitement as she got ready for the annual ball. Sitting in front of her English-style vanity table, three mirrors were angled toward her, allowing her to see herself from three different vantage points. Eddy, one of the younger and more inexperienced slaves in the house, fit Celia into a cream-colored dress. She started pinning the dress as Marlene walked into the room.

"Is everything ready for the ball tonight?" Celia asked.

"Yes, Miss Celia," Marlene answered. "I've seen to it myself."

"Good, I don't want any problems. There are going to be a lot of big people here tonight, so make sure everything runs good."

"Yes, Miss."

As Eddy struggled to better fit and pin the dress, Celia and Marlene looked at each other in the mirror.

"You look beautiful," Marlene said.

"When I want your opinion, I will ask for it!"

"Yes, Miss Celia."

"Marlene, have you ever wished you were white?" Celia asked, sounding bored. "Life would probably be so much easier for you. It must be hard for you now. You are not ugly like them others, but you're not as pretty as some of my white friends."

"Black is all I know; I wouldn't know what to do if I was white," Marlene said, watching Celia jump and pause before becoming silent. Infuriated, Celia glared at Eddy, who looked up helplessly.

"How dare you!" Celia yelled. "You pricked me on purpose!"

"I'm sorry—"

"Marlene, call the overseers right now," Celia ordered, looking back at Eddy. "You need to be taught a lesson."

"I'm sure it was a mistake," Marlene offered. "She didn't mean to hurt you."

"Please, Miss Celia!" Eddy pleaded.

"Marlene, call them right now, or you will be joining her!"

As Eddy dropped to her knees, crying, Marlene briskly walked into the hallway. She looked around and saw one of the overseers further down the hall. Pausing as if she were checking, she returned to the room. "I couldn't find him."

"Eric! Eric! Come here at once!" Celia screamed for the houseman.

"Yes, Miss Celia?" Eric asked, nervously glancing around.

"Take Eddy to see the overseer. Tell him she needs to be taught a lesson. Make sure he takes her outside and shows her some manners."

He paused, until Celia yelled, "Now!"

"Come with me, Eddy," he whispered, reluctantly kneeling to help her up.

"No, please, I can do better," Eddy cried hysterically. "Please don't—not that. I can do better."

Marlene looked away as Eric pulled Eddy out of the room.

"So, how do I look?" Celia calmly asked Marlene.

***

Outside, Eddy was dragged toward the barn. Fighting and crying all the way, she was no match for the overseer.

"Please, no! I will be good!"

Overseer Jean dragged her to the back of the barn, pulling her over to a post and tying her arms to it. "Eddy, when will you learn?" he asked.

"But I didn't do nothing wrong; it was an accident!"

Jean placed a cattle rod on top of a small lit flame in the center of the room. The rod began to heat up, eventually glowing bright red. "No one can hear you scream in here," he told her, smiling. Tearing at the back of her dress, he exposed her back, already bruised and scarred from earlier beatings. He walked over to the small heater and grabbed the handle of the rod. "You have got to learn to be more careful."

She screamed in pain as he placed the iron on her skin.

From her hiding spot in front of the barn, Marlene cringed with each of Eddy's screams. Almost fifteen minutes later, Jean walked out and closed the door behind him. After Marlene watched him walk away, she ran into the large, dark barn, looking for Eddy.

"Eddy? Eddy? Where are you?" she loudly whispered. Turning around, she saw Eddy slumped over a table, her back bleeding badly.

"Oh my Lord!" Marlene shouted, rushing over. "What did he do?"

Still hysterically screaming, Eddy didn't realize the ordeal is over. Marlene held her up, trying to comfort her. "I'm here. He's gone. It's all right."

"I can't take it. I wish I was dead," Eddy said, gradually calming down in Marlene's arms. "It'd be better than this."

CHAPTER TEN

Chapter 10

Dedicated to Lunsford Lane and the Amistad Mutiny

Seven Years Later

Birds still sang outside the big house. Shades of light still streamed through beautiful trees, and sunlight pierced the clouds. John ran through a beautiful open field next to a hill and small stream. Water cascaded over jagged rocks, slowly falling into a small pond below.

"You're going to get us in trouble," Ellie said, chasing after him.

"Your mom is going to be mighty mad if we are late. The ball's tonight."

"I know how to handle her," John said, reaching for her hand. At nineteen years old, he was on the cusp of manhood.

"We should be getting back," Ellie says.

"In a minute," John said coyly.

"Come on! Last time we got in trouble," Ellie said. "We couldn't see each other for a week."

"We'll get there. I just wanted to show you this place. I used to come here when I was a kid. Uncle Joe used to catch fish in this pond. He said it was magical. Whatever I wished for would come true."

Ellie looked out over the water, becoming more relaxed. "It's peaceful and quiet."

"Ever thought about leaving?" John asked.

"All the time," Ellie said, smiling.

"Why don't you?"

"I wouldn't know where to go or how to leave."

"We could leave together."

"As fast as you can run," Ellie said, "I'd hold you back. You could outrun anyone. I couldn't keep up."

"One day I want to take you away to a place like this, but where we are free," he said.

"I'll be happy wherever you are," Ellie said. "So, what did you wish for?"

Dropping to one knee, John kept his back straight as he looked up into her eyes. "Ellie, I love you. I want to spend the rest of my life with you. Will you marry me?"

Taking a deep breath, Ellie covered her smile as tears welled in her eyes. "Yes."

John embraced her and pulled her down to the grass. They rolled around, laughing. John kissed her and howled with joy. He grabbed her hand, and they ran toward Main Street on their way back to the plantation. Three young white men stood on the side of road, seeing the happy couple.

"Where do you think you're going?" Donald Corey, the group's leader, asked, angrily walking toward them.

"Back to the plantation."

"You're not freed, are you?"

"No."

"Lucky you said that," Donald said with a cold, sinister smile. "Because if you weren't someone's property, you'd be dead. Don't you know, your kind ain't welcomed in these parts. You don't walk on the sidewalk. Get in the street!"

As John sized him up, Ellie grabbed his hand. John reluctantly followed Ellie into the street. The group laughed as they walked off. John looked over at Ellie and managed an awkward smile as they continued down the road, now in the street. "I didn't want to walk on that hard sidewalk anyway," he said unconvincingly.

"Wherever you go, I will follow," Ellie said with a half-smile. For the rest of that walk up the road, they never let go of each other's hands. Sometimes it was hard to keep their dignity, but Ellie made it a lot easier.

Farther ahead, John and Ellie saw a group of slaves on an auction block. A crowd of men stood around bidding on them. Ellie began to cry.

"What will you give me for these slaves?" the slaver eagerly shouted.

***

John and Ellie's wedding day was clear and sunny. They walked down a small path near the river, hand in hand. Marlene looked on in tears. Several other slaves surrounded them. Two men lowered a broom and placed it under John and Ellie. They jumped over it, symbolizing their marriage. Carl looked on from the distance. He left the wedding with his mind made up.

A few hours later, Carl, now eighteen, passed Celia on the porch of the big house, with his bags packed.

"Where do you think you are going?" Celia asked, looking at the bags with disdain.

"To join the North and fight."

"You will do no such thing."

"You have always said to do the right thing, but do you? You think those people were put on this earth to serve us. We stole them and brought them here. I've made my mind up, and there's nothing you can do to stop me."

"Carl, your brother is fighting right now for the South. How can you do that?"

"What we are doing to those people is wrong," Carl yelled back.

"They have a right to live the same way we do!"

"Carl, you are not going anywhere! Who cares about those slaves? You are my son!"

"You can't control me anymore. I make my own decisions. That's your problem—you try to control everything. You treat everyone here like your property. Well, I am not your property—I am your son." Carl walked over to his mother, stopped, and then turned to leave.

"I will write, Mother," he said more calmly. "This I have to do."

"Carl, you come back here! If you leave now, I'll disown you! You have no mother!"

"Never really did anyway." He walked off as she watched for a few minutes before going back into the house.

"Marlene! Marlene! Where are you?" she called out, furiously. When she saw Marlene on the floor, cleaning, she marched over and waited for her to look up.

"Yes, Miss?" Marlene answered.

"You—I know you put him up to this!" Celia yelled, pointing her finger in Marlene's face.

"Miss Celia, what?"

"My son is going to fight for the North because of you! You filled his mind with lies against me," Celia screamed, grabbing her by the shirt.

"I told him nothing!"

"First my husband and now my sons! I want you out of my house now! You go and see the overseer. I lose my son, and you lose yours!" Expecting Marlene to beg for her life, Celia stared at her and waited.

Marlene quietly walked out and headed toward the back of the house. She slowly walked toward the barn, where most of the slaves were punished, and closed the door behind her.

The next day John and Ellie waited for Marlene in front of the big house. As soon as Marlene stepped outside, Ellie held her tight.

"It's your job to take care of him now," Marlene told her.

John waited by the carriage, with tears in his eyes. He walked over, hugged Marlene, and broke down crying. Marlene wiped his face with a handkerchief.

"All right, stop that," she said, intensely looking into his eyes. "You must protect yourself and Ellie now that I'm not here. I want you to have this." She handed him a handkerchief. "It's the only thing that's mine in this world. I want you to keep it and think of me—something to remember me by."

"I don't want you to go," John cried.

"One day I'll be back. Miss Celia is just sending me away for a while. Remember, no matter what, I love you, and I'm always with you."

"I just want to thank you for giving me a life worth living," John said, overcome with grief.

"You be good." Marlene smiled, fighting back tears. Not looking back, she stepped up into the carriage, and John cried uncontrollably as it took off. As it picked up speed, John chased after it. Marlene tried hard not to watch. He continued to run until he could no longer see the carriage.

She never came back. John was happy she was sent up North. Miss Celia's husband seen to it, but it was the last time he saw her. Years later, Miss Celia's husband said she had died of a broken heart.

CHAPTER
ELEVEN

Chapter 11

Dedicated to J. Vance Lewis and the Woman Suffrage Movement

Three Years Later

A cork popped, and the champagne bubbled over. Long lines of carriages were parked out front. A bevy of guests eagerly waited by the entrance. The North was fighting the South in what many were calling the Civil War, so this year's annual ball would be different. Several distinguished men entered dressed in their best black suits, while the women were dressed in some of the most elaborate dresses of the day. Servants in front of the house took coats. One guest snarled and grabbed his coat, displeased with a slave for touching it. A carriage came to a halt, allowing a small group of soldiers to ride past on their way to the front. A large group of well-dressed women tried not to look at the soldiers, their uneasiness masked by a defiant belief that things would never change, that slavery would never end.

Inside, guests congregated in the foyer. They began to mingle and make small talk. A band of performers played Southern music. Male servants dressed in black-and-white outfits offered tall glasses of champagne.

Ellie stood outside the window of the large, elegantly decorated ballroom, swaying to the music. John walked up behind her, embracing her at the waist.

"You startled me," Ellie jumped, smiling.

"How do you like it?"

"I love it."

"My mother used to sit me outside this window whenever they played music."

"It's wonderful," Ellie said, somberly.

"I miss her so much," John said, followed by a long pause. "Want to dance?"

"Like them? I don't know how," Ellie said.

"Just follow me."

"I couldn't."

John took her hand and did a choppy box step, which slowly improved and they both laughed together.

"I like this," Ellie said.

"Every year they had this ball, my mother would open the windows so I could listen. I used to dance out here by myself and think one thing."

"What?"

"I wished for someone to dance with, and here you are."

"I knew you were special," Ellie said, smiling. "Just didn't know how much."

As they continued to dance, the music stopped, and everyone went to the window. John grabbed Ellie's hand and hid under a windowsill moments before fireworks exploded across the sky. There were fireworks back inside as well. A loud commotion greeted General Conley's grand entrance. He was dressed in his Confederate army uniform. The lights from the candlelit chandelier caused the medals on his chest to sparkle.

"Good evening to all—good evening," Conley said.

Keith, a guest who owned slaves, looked over at Conley. "You give them hell! Make sure they know the South will not be kicked around!" he yelled in Conley's direction. "We will never yield to the North."

Conley held up his hands. "My friends, the South will never fall. We will defeat the North and end any attempts to end slavery. Lincoln's army is no match for the Confederate army. It is a God-given right for everyone to own slaves."

"How can you be so sure?" Keith asked. "Isn't the North strong?"

"We have rights and righteousness on our side. With God behind us, nothing can stop the South." And with that, Conley confidently nodded to the crowd gathered around him and proceeded into the dining room.

Although many eyes were still fixed on him, Celia was determined to make her own grand entrance from the top of one of the two long, winding staircases that led into the foyer. Down below, Michael smiled and clapped with delight as she walked down the stairs and over to Conley, kissing him on the cheek.

"General Conley, I'm so happy you could make it," she said.

"Judging from your presence here, we must be doing well with the war."

"I assure you we are," he said. "I am awaiting good news from the front. Once it gets here, I will share it with everyone."

Later, in the ballroom, as several men and women danced the night away, Conley took a drink, a concerned look on his face.

Several soldiers marched through the door, and once they spotted Conley, one rushed to him with a letter. The soldier's grim expression already told Conley what he was about to read. Conley got up and abruptly started to leave. Celia watched from across the room. "Leaving so soon?" she asked, keeping up with his brisk pace in her heels.

"I'm sorry, but I must go."

"Is everything all right?" Celia asked. "My sons are fighting in this war."

"Things are not going as well as we thought, but we will prevail. Now, if you will excuse me …" As he leaves, a soldier continued talking in his ear.

"What's happening?" Conley asked.

"It's not good, sir," the soldier answered. "We are losing on both fronts."

"Get my horse. I will head to the front. We will make our stand there."

CHAPTER
TWELVE

Chapter 12

Dedicated to Moses Roper and the *North Star*

Ranging between ages fifteen and fifty, thousands of soldiers from both the North and the South moved slowly toward an open field. The winds had changed; it blew in a different direction.

Several units of the Northern army, including former slaves, stood ready to engage in battle, with cold stares and apprehension on their faces as they marched forward.

General Foley rode over on horseback, sizing up his men and gazing across the field. He steadied his horse and readied his troops for battle. Once he signaled for his troops to advance, a battle cry is heard, followed by a loud thunder. Both armies charged. The pounding footsteps mixed with gunfire and cannon fire. After the two sides clashed in an epic test of will, the area could only be described as hell on earth. Total chaos and mayhem ensued as each side struggled to defeat the other in a maddening frenzy.

When the battle had ended, an eerie silence fell on the field. A light mist left from the gunpowder blew in the wind. Hundreds of bodies littered the field. The surviving soldiers walked among the carnage, looking for familiar faces.

After hours of searching for his brother, Martin Gray, one of the few surviving Confederate soldiers, shuffled over to a body lying facedown in the field. He recognized the jacket.

Turning the body over, he sobbed uncontrollably, kneeling and removing his hat.

"Wake up! Come on," he cried softly, shaking him. "What am I going to tell Mom?"

He picked up his brother's lifeless body, gently placed it over his shoulder, and walked off through the decimated field.

CHAPTER
THIRTEEN

Chapter 13

Dedicated to Fountain Hughes and the Seneca Falls Convention

It was voting day on Main Street. Slaves were driven in wagons to a voting area. Several white men stood on the sides of the road, watching the slaves who came down from the wagon to line up to vote. "If you know what's good for you, vote for the South," snarled a Confederate soldier handing out fliers. "The South has been good to you. What would you do without slavery? Where will you go? Where will you work?"

Joe walked over and stood next to an elderly man who tried to read a sign. "They know most of us can't read," the man said, confused. Looking around, he saw Joe standing behind him.

"Excuse me, can you help me? I don't know what to do. Master says if I vote for the North, he will beat me, but if I don't, we will always be slaves. I can't read."

"You have to do what's right," Joe says. "It is your vote. We don't even count as a vote, since they say we are three-fifths of a man."

"If you and I both vote together, then we count for more than a man."

Billy John, a Confederate soldier, saw Joe talking to the other slaves and grew enraged. He signaled to another soldier, and they approached Joe.

"Here is Joe, always with something to say," Billy said sinisterly. "They should have cut your tongue out like we done our slaves."

"We don't have any rights, but one—the right to vote," Joe said.

"It's not even a full vote. They can vote for whoever they like."

"Now, Joe, there you go talking again. One day someone may have to come pay you a visit to shut you up!"

"If any man were to come knocking at my door, they would find me answering it."

Angered by Joe's defiance, Billy stepped toward him as a soldier grabbed Billy's arm. Several slaves looked on. Billy looked at the hand of the soldier on his arm and pulled away. "See you around," he said before walking away.

Joe stared him down. "Anytime."

"You talk back to them?" the elderly man in line asked Joe. "Don't you know who they are?"

"I don't care who they are. If we don't stand up to this, we are always going to be prisoners. I fought for this country."

"You better lower your voice before they hear you."

"I am tired of lowering my voice. We are men; they should treat us like men. We helped build this country, and they need to start respecting us."

Joe got out of line and walked toward Henderson, an overweight man and the only person staffing the voting area. He took his time as he collected the votes.

"Excuse me, sir, I would like to vote."

"Get back in line."

"I was only allowed fifteen minutes to come here to vote."

"Get back in line now."

"But, sir, you're not even taking the votes."

"I said get back in line. I'm not going to tell you again."

Joe defiantly walked over a voting booth and picked up a ballot.

"Put it down." Henderson grabbed Joe's hand, and they locked into a stare. Scared, sensing Joe's strength, he backed down and retreated to get help. Joe continued taking a ballot and a pencil, carefully looking at the sheet.

A few minutes later, Henderson returned with several Confederate soldiers—and Billy.

"Put the pencil down," Henderson repeated.

"Let me vote, and I'll be on my way," Joe said.

"You just don't listen," Billy said, shaking his head.

As Joe walked to place his ballot in the box, Billy grabbed him from behind. Keeping his sights firmly on the voting box, Joe struggled forward to get his ballot into the box, knowing the power that vote had. It was all slaves had in this country, and he was not about to let anyone take it from him. Several Confederate soldiers converged on him and started beating him with sticks. With several slaves looking on, horrified, Joe dropped to one knee, still struggling to place his ballot in the box, eventually falling to the ground. While on the ground, he was brutally beaten, kicked, and humiliated. His ballot fell to the ground, too, and blew into a corner.

Joe struggled to free himself. He was picked up and dragged outside. Several slaves looked on as he was pulled off the property, some with tears in their eyes, but they continued to wait in line.

Billy laughed with delight. "Look at you now, boy."

That night the elderly man reached the front of the line. He walked over to the booth, took a ballot, and checked the box to end slavery. He saw Uncle Joe's ballot on the floor. Dropping his hat, he stooped down to pick it up before placing it in the box.

Joe had finally fallen asleep next to his wife after thinking about his day, still in pain. If he were still awake, he would have seen the door to their room open. In the dark, he would have been able to make out the figure of a burly man with a white sheet over his head slowly but methodically approaching the bed. He may have seen the knife and the rope in the intruder's hands.

Joe's wife woke up and rolled over, vaguely sensing something was wrong. She felt cold and walked over to the window. As she closed it, a figure came from behind her, wrapped his hand around her mouth, and pulled her out of the house. Joe was still fast asleep. Another man entered and walked over to Joe. He paused and walked out.

Outside, the two men loaded Joe's wife into the back of a wagon.

"Why didn't you kill him?" the man in the sheet asked in a muffled voice.

"I want him to suffer," Billy answered. "After what we do to this one tonight, he'll be as good as dead anyway."

They hopped into the back of the wagon and drove off.

CHAPTER

FOURTEEN

Chapter 14

Dedicated to Harriet Tubman, *Uncle Tom's Cabin*, and
Migratory Workers

Joe was having a nightmare about his wife. He tossed back and forth before waking up in a cold sweat. He looked over and realized she was gone. He searched the room, still a little groggy. "Lucile? Lucile?" Nobody answered. He got out of bed and looked around the one-room shack. Noticing the window was open and the front door ajar, a grim feeling came over him. "Oh God, no." Grabbing his hat, he ran out of the house, slamming the door behind him. The forest was silent except for the sounds of a howling wolf in the distance. Joe ran full speed through the woods. As he stumbled through the deep forest, his fears deepened, and his anger grew. "Lucile! Lucile!" he hollered, holding back tears. When he looked over his shoulder, he lost his footing and fell down a steep hill toward a small creek, landing on a tree trunk with a loud thump.

He gathered himself, tried to get his bearings, and he saw his worst fears realized. He dropped to his knees and sobbed. There above him, perched high in a large tree, Lucile hung from a rope, completely nude. After he brought her down, Joe carefully took his shirt off and wrapped it around her nude body. Crying uncontrollably, he wiped Lucile's face, as evidence of her ordeal was visible all over her body. Her face was badly bruised and unrecognizable. Leaning forward, he kissed her gently. "Lucile, wake up. Lucile?" He lifted her body and carried her off into the forest.

Over on Main Street, Billy sat out front with two other men. They were laughing, passing around a bottle of whiskey. Billy took one last swig and walked off, leaving the other men behind. As he inched up the block, he began to sense someone was following him, but he paid it no mind. As he got closer to the road, he saw Joe standing in front of him. "What are you doing here?"

Joe ignored him.

"What do you want?" Billy seemed nervous.

Joe moved slowly toward him, his hand firmly clasped, his teeth clenched.

"Cat got your tongue?"

Joe wondered whether anyone could smile as sinisterly as Billy.

"Oh, you must have seen your wife. Funny thing, she just wouldn't shut up. So we had to choke her, but before we did, I made sure we had our way with her."

Joe moved in closer.

"What? Do you want to call the sheriff? I'll tell my father to stop by. I'm sure he'll believe you over his own son. Or better yet, I'll confess. How much time do you think I'll get for killing one of you?"

Joe stood inches away from Billy's face.

"Three or four days in jail," Billy yelled. "Now, why don't you be a good boy and get out of my face!"

Joe grabbed him by the throat, smiling. Billy was no match for Joe, who outweighed him by seventy pounds.

"Get off me!" Billy gasped, trying to catch his breath.

Joe continued to strangle Billy until he was nearly dead, and then he let him go.

Billy sank to the ground, gasping for air. "You. Are. Going. To. Pay. For. That," Billy panted. "It's good you came to your senses."

"No! I want you to suffer—just like my wife." Joe grabbed him by the legs and dragged him into the woods. The following night a small mob gathered on Main Street. They carried torches and rope. John watched from a distance. That was the first time he had seen the mob.

Sheriff Ray—an extremist and overweight man with a heavy Southern drawl—walked out of the shadows. "My son is missing. Let everyone know," Ray said intensely. "Whoever did this is going to pay!"

Ray's assistant, Bob, suddenly joined him." They say your boy had a run-in with Joe."

"If it's him, he won't make it out of the South alive!"

"What are we going to do? His master isn't going to be happy."

"I don't care."

Johnson, a friend of Ray's, joined Ray and Bob. Of the three of them, he was the only one who looked excited. "I rounded everyone up. Let's get the dogs out. He's probably on foot. We should speak to the law."

"I am the law," Ray growled. "Now let's move."

"I heard they took to his wife something awful," Johnson said.

"Shut up!" Ray interrupted. "I don't care how you do it. Find him and bring him to me."

Ray aggressively stormed off, the group following behind him, searching the woods. Reluctantly, Johnson followed the group, struggling to catch up.

It was a witch hunt. All who could be found were found guilty.

CHAPTER

FIFTEEN

William Still

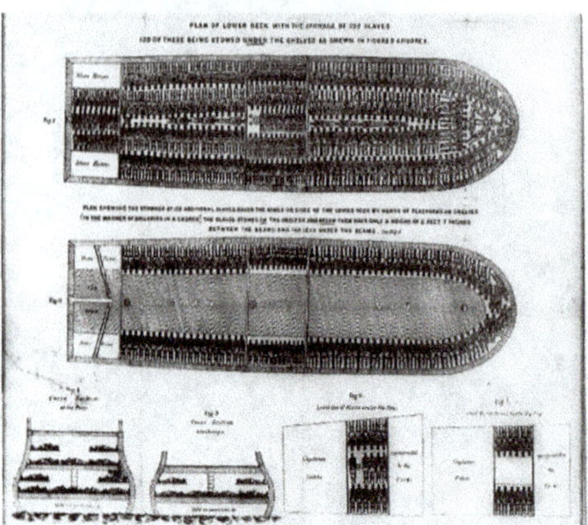

Chapter 15

Dedicated to William Still and Slaves Who Survived
and Perished

In the forest, a light mist came off the trees. The moon quickly rose, providing the night's only illumination. Four men on horses rode in formation through the dense forest. Their faces were obscured. Several slaves ran for their lives as the men on horseback closed in and caught up to them, eventually overtaking them. The slaves surrendered.

Three men with sheets over their heads converged on a small area with four mud buildings—the slave quarters. They broke in and pulled out several slaves. The more the slaves struggled, the more they suffered. One of the men, the leader, wore a pure-white sheet that the moonlight made look even whiter. He rushed in, grabbing more slaves, aggressively pulling them out of their beds.

"Get them—all of them," he instructed in a hurried tone. "They all are going to pay. Tonight is hell night."

The captured slaves were led into the forest. A large fire burned in the barn, which was surrounded by many men. As the slaves looked on, Ray grabbed one of the men and dragged him to the fire. With the help of two others, he pushed him into the fire as the man screamed and struggled.

"You have to learn your place in the world," Ray yelled, enjoying himself. "This is our country, our world. In it, you are nothing. When will you learn? My son is missing; he may be dead. I can't bring him back, but I sure as hell can kill every one of you. I will kill everyone here if I don't find my son." As another person was tossed into the fire, Ray looked on in delight.

The next morning John knew exactly where to find Joe. When he reached the river, he ran to him. Joe tensed before realizing it was John.

"Uncle Joe, are you, all right?"

"She's gone. I put her in the water. I didn't want to bury her in this place, so I placed her in the water."

"They're looking for you. What are you going to do?"

Ignoring John's question, Joe whispered angrily, "I can't believe it—what they did to her."

John grabbed his arm. "You got to run."

"I am tired of running—tired of this godforsaken place," Joe yelled, sobbing. "I want to be free. I can't take it. Maybe they did her a favor, letting her spirit go free. I only hope God can forgive me."

"Forgive you for what?"

"Joining her. Life without her isn't worth living." He walked toward the lake as John looked on.

"Don't go! Please, Uncle Joe!"

Joe continued walking until the water reached his neck. John did nothing but cry from the shore. When he dipped under the water, he was halfway across the pond.

As the sun set in the distance, John looked toward where Joe went under, teary-eyed and silent. He must have stayed there for hours, looking at the water, hoping Joe, who came to believe it was better to die a man than to live as a slave, would come back.

A horse-drawn coach drove up to the big house that night. Martin stepped down from it, carrying his brother's body. When Celia ran outside, she dropped to her knees.

"No, God. Why? Not my son!" she cried.

Martin looked at her stoically. "You free all of them in the field tonight. If you don't, you'll lose another son by morning." He walked away, still cradling his brother.

In the slave quarters, John was awakened by several men who pulled him out of bed and took him outside, where he was joined by several other slaves. They were lined up against the wall.

Instead of freedom, Celia sold her slaves to Sneely, the local slaver. She wanted them to suffer for her son's death.

They were pushed into caged wagons. The chains around their necks and ankles were so tight that they could barely breathe. Celia and Michael looked on from the porch of the big house.

"Do we have to do this?" Michael asked.

"I am not losing another son. One died for them, and I want them to suffer. I don't want any of them on my property."

"Why sell them? Why not free them?"

"We will keep the house ones, but everyone in the field is going. Besides, why should we lose our money on them? At least this way we get something back for them."

John stared out the back window of the wagon leaving the Gray's plantation—the only home he's ever known.

CHAPTER
SIXTEEN

Chapter 16

Dedicated to Frederick Douglass and the
Emancipation Proclamation

Once the wagons were safely inside a huge front gate, an overseer sternly locked the gate behind them. Another large house sat at the end of a winding road, and the wagons stopped in front of it.

The overseers opened the wagon doors, directing the slaves to come out, sticks in hand, grim expressions on their faces. When John walked out, he first noticed a tower and a huge wall at the end of the path. He heard screams all around them.

Robert Sneely appeared, walking outside from behind a bright light. He was known as one of Baton Rouge's shrewdest slavers. Robert walked over to John and looked him in the face, grabbing and poking him like cattle. "This one is for the field."

He was evil—the devil himself. He had several children with slaves he brutally beat, calling them all abominations. Using the largest of the male slaves to control the others, he felt punishment should be delivered by a strong hand.

"Listen up, because I am only going to say this once," he yelled.

"You are my property. Your last name will be Sneely. This is your home. I expect nothing but hard work. You step out of line once, it will be severe. Twice, and you will wish you were never born. Do I make myself clear?"

His son Richard sidled up beside him. Richard was just as cocky as his father, but more brutal. With his father, it was business. Richard enjoyed whipping young slave girls and putting them down. "You heard my father," he yelled. "Move!"

Richard grabbed Ellie's arm and smiled at her.

"You go into the house."

"I want to work in the field," Ellie said.

"Move," Richard said, not finished with her yet. "Get her out of my sight."

All the slaves were taken to the side of a road and branded on their arms with a hot iron. A full moon rose just over the horizon. Stars shimmered in the frigid night air. An icy mist covered the trees. John looked toward the sky, closed his eyes, and placed his hands together as if praying. Winter was setting in, and it promised to be a particularly harsh one.

The unrelenting pace of the new plantation had immediately taken its toll on the slaves. As he picked cotton, John tried to keep his hands warm by rubbing them as frequently as possible. His skin blistered, and his hands started to crack and bleed.

While Ellie cleaned inside the house, she constantly looked outside the window, wondering how John was doing. Richard walked into the kitchen, ogling Ellie.

"You are too beautiful to be cleaning floors," he said, taking an apple from a bowl on a side table and slowly biting into it.

"I have no problem doing it."

He propped his feet up on the table and leaned back in his chair. "Well, if you ever want a better life, you had better be nice to me, and I will see to it."

Ellie kept her eyes on the floor. "I don't mind the kitchen."

"Kitchen? That's not what I had in mind." He smiled and grabbed her arm. Pulling her close to him, he coldly stared into her eyes. "You have a husband out in the field. Life for him can be difficult. He could have an accident or wind up seriously hurt. If you're good to me, maybe I can help him. You think about it." He ran his fingers through Ellie's hair and smiled. He walked away smiling, humming to himself.

The sun had set, and John still worked in the fields of Sneely Manor with Daniel and Paul. Daniel was small and slow. John looked over to Paul. "I can't take it any longer. We shouldn't have to live like this."

"This is the way it is," Paul said.

"They are fighting up North to free the slaves."

"You better be quiet," Daniel said in a low voice, overhearing the two men talk. "If Overseer Frank hears you speak like that, he will take a whip to you."

"Has anyone ever escaped?" John continued.

"If you could fly, you could go over the wall," Daniel said.

"What?"

"Don't mind him," Paul kindly interrupted. "He's a little sick in the head. I've been here for years. It's easy to run through the marsh if you can get over the wall. You just have to watch for the dogs and the overseers."

"That it?" John asked, the wheels turning in his head.

"If you get to the swamp, you got to watch for the alligators. To make it worse, they burned all the trees around the property, so it's hard to hide," Paul said.

"If you had wings, you could fly," Daniel said, laughing and shaking his head.

"So, why have that big wall?" John asked.

"It's almost impossible to get over it. When one boy made it to the top, they raised it a foot," Paul said.

"Mister Sneely said if anyone could jump that high, they deserve to be free," Daniel added, smiling.

"I can jump high," John said, realizing he could get over it.

"Are you crazy? Don't even think it. The man who made it to the top was shot in the back—dead."

"Once over, they can't find you, because they don't own that property. They couldn't burn the trees down, so there lots of hiding places," Daniel said, giving John more hope.

"It doesn't matter. It would take a miracle to get over the wall and then survive in those woods," Paul counseled.

Overseers Frank and Hawkins marched toward them.

"What do you think you're doing?" Frank yelled. "Get back to work." He slammed the stick, hitting the wall.

Hawkins motioned to Daniel. "All but this one. Come here, Daniel. What were they talking about?"

Paul stared at John.

"Nothing," Daniel said.

"You sure?" Hawkins smiled. "You wouldn't want us to go get the whip."

"Never mind," Frank laughed. "Say, why don't you show us a dance step?

"Yeah, show us one of those steps you do," Hawkins chimed in.

Daniel reluctantly started to dance. They looked on, laughing.

After a hard day working the field, John sat on the floor of his quarters. He pulled out a stolen piece of paper and began to write a letter to Ellie.

The next morning Ellie cleaned the floors of the kitchen. One of the slaves dropped the letter onto the floor and walked out. Ellie looked both ways before quickly picking it up. She walked over to a closet to read it. She saw that it was from John and began to smile.

You are with me always. I see you every night in my dreams. I must do something. Remember, I love you always, and I'm always with you.

Ellie started to cry. She took the letter, placed it in her shirt, and went back to the kitchen floor, now cleaning it with a smile.

The rain slammed against the metal rooftop of the slaves' quarters. John's bed was an old tattered blanket placed on top of the dirt floor. Insects scurried around his head while he slept. Awakened by a disturbance outside, he rose to his feet and walked to the front door. Paul walked behind him. Slowly opening the front door, John looked both ways to check for overseers. He saw several men gathered together in the distance, talking for a few seconds before running in opposite directions.

"What's going on?" John whispered loudly.

"Sounds like someone's trying to escape."

John quickly walked back to his sleeping area, looking determined, realizing this may be his only chance.

"John, where are you going?"

Picking up his mother's handkerchief, John grabbed a blanket to cover him.

"Tell Ellie I love her, and I'll be back for her."

"What are you doing?" Paul cried. "You're going to get yourself killed!"

Daniel woke up to see John packing. "He's gone crazy," he stuttered.

"You know, Mister Sneely will take a switch to you for opening that door," Paul said.

"Quiet—I'm leaving."

"Where are you going?"

"Any place is better than here."

"To do what?"

"They are fighting right now so slaves like us can be free—North against the South, and I am going to join them."

"Don't leave," Daniel pleaded.

"I have to go, but I will be back—I promise." John nodded at Daniel and briskly walked out of the front door. Paul sat down in the middle of the room and folded his legs. Daniel sat cross-legged on the cold floor, nervously hugging and rocking himself, jumping at the slightest sound outside.

Looking both ways, John turned a corner and headed toward the fields. He looked at the wall and paused for a moment. "Impossible?" he asked himself. "If I go this way, they'll catch me. There's got to be another way." He searched around the immediate area, looking for rope. Startled by the sound of a barking dog, he froze. As the dog began to bark more wildly, he looked around, but the dog was out of his view. Hearing footsteps behind him, he moved more slowly. The sounds picked up as the footsteps drew closer. He quickly swerved around as a light from the tower flashed in his direction.

From his lookout booth, Overseer Frank heard the dogs barking and swung a large spotlight in the direction of John. He got excited when he was able to make out John's body. "We have ourselves another runner." He motioned to Overseer Will. "Sound the alarm."

Overseer Will stepped over to a crank alarm. He grabbed the handle on the wheel and began cranking it. As he picked up speed, a loud siren wailed.

"Over there! There he is!" Frank yelled as he saw John's futile efforts to hide from the spotlight. "We got one trying to run!"

John finally managed to elude the light by hiding behind a small shack. More lights from around the plantation lit up. In the distance, the alarm grew louder—the telltale signal for an escape attempt.

In his booth, Overseer Frank fumbled for the keys to open a locked cabinet, from which he pulls out two double-barreled shotguns. He took one and tossed the other over to Overseer Will. "Let's go. I don't want them to have all of the fun."

From behind the shack, John saw five slaves—two females and three males—running toward the fields. Shortly after, the overseers chased after them. Realizing he couldn't escape into the fields, John turned and looked toward the wall. But when he turned, it was not the wall he saw. Rather, it was six-four, three-hundred-pound Overseer Ridge towering two feet away. Ridge threw John against the wall. As John struggled, Ridge fiercely lunged, his massive frame landing on top of him. John winced in pain, but he raised his fists to defend himself. As Ridge swung wildly, John swiftly kicked him in the groin and ran into the darkness, hoping that Ridge would stay slumped over on the ground.

Across the field, another group of overseers opened the dog cages. After Overseer Frank grabbed one of the dogs, it stopped in his tracks and pulled him in the opposite direction.

"What's wrong, boy?" Frank asked, hopeful. "Come on. Let's go."

The dog, now in a frenzy, aggressively pulled Frank in a specific direction. Frank followed, looking around. Seeing John, he gritted his teeth.

"There he is!" he shouted. "Come on!"

When he saw Frank running toward him, John also noticed an oil lamp on the ground across from him. He ran over, grabbed the lamp, and threw it into a small barn that stored cotton. Dashing away from the fire that quickly erupted, Frank released the dog. The large German shepherd headed straight for John at full speed.

As John ran, his eyes darted all over the field. When he heard gunfire and saw flashes of light, it was even clearer that escape through the field was not an option. Hundreds of trees had long since burned down, and the remains of numerous slaves had been scattered across the ground as a message to others trying to escape.

He looked again at the wall. He threw the blanket off and ran as fast as he could toward it. Frank watched John's every move. Swinging his rifle off his shoulder, he dropped to one knee, steadied the weapon, and placed John in the gun's sights.

As a foggy mist rose from the ground, several of the escaping slaves navigated through the carcasses of fallen trees to evade gunfire. But the dogs caught up with them. A male slave, running while holding the hand of a female slave, was shot in the back. She stopped as he signaled for her to continue running and struggled to pull him up, not realizing he was dead. She knelt and held him as the dogs closed in, resigned to her fate.

Once Frank decided he had a clear shot at John, two dogs closed in near his legs as he climbed. Totally focused, John didn't look back. One dog lunged for his leg, barely missing him, but John didn't break his stride.

His finger on the trigger, Frank was ready to pull it, smiling slightly. "Almost made it. Pity," he said to himself, shaking his head.

"Nowhere to go now. Goodbye." As he fired, Daniel knocked him to the ground from behind. The shotgun fired but missed John. Daniel struggled on top of Frank, preventing him from getting the gun that had fallen to the ground.

"Fly, fly, fly!" Daniel screamed in John's direction.

John leaped into the air toward the wall as the house on fire exploded in the background. As the fire raged behind them, Overseer Frank looked up and saw John holding on to the top of the wall with one hand. The dogs at the base of the wall jumped and barked relentlessly. Daniel looked up at John and smiles lightly as tears streamed down his face. Frank looked up at John, too, more stunned than choked with emotion. "That's impossible. nobody can do that," he said.

He spotted his gun a few feet to the right of him and lunged for it while Daniel, who had loosened his grip, was more focused on John. He quickly cocked the barrel as John struggled to grasp the top of the wall with his other hand. With great effort, he successfully brought his other hand over. He pulled himself up and over just as Frank fired another shot, barely missing him.

CHAPTER
SEVENTEEN

Chapter 17

Dedicated to Lucy Delaney and Benjamin Franklin

Tall grass surrounded John. He had walked for several days. Awakened by the sound of horses and fearing it was the overseers, he prepared to run. John saw an army brigade marching and riding past him. He ran in their direction, waving his hands. Captain Thomas looked over at John, curiously.

"Sir, begging your pardon," John said, saluting him. "I want to join."

"You? Serve?" Captain Thomas asked in a Southern accent. "What can you do?"

"My Uncle served, and if you give me a chance, I'd like to help too—that is, if you can use an extra hand. The plantation I ran from is mistreating the slaves there. All I want to do is help them."

"You haven't heard?" the captain asked. "The North won the war. The South has surrendered, and slavery is over—you are free."

Losing his footing for a second, John composed himself. "Free? I can't believe it. The plantation I just left is still using slaves. What can you do to help them?"

"Maybe they haven't got word. Come with us; I will talk to them. We need all the help we can get. Get this man a uniform," the Captain said, looking around and saluting John. "You are part of the Union army now. Carry on, Soldier."

Gary, a wide-eyed black solider, handed John an old jacket, holding it open for John to slip into. He placed a hat on his head. As the unit started to move out, John fell in line behind them, smiling.

"Can you believe we are free?" Gary asked as they marched.

Overseer Frank hurried over to Robert and Richard Sneely. From the expression on his face, they already knew what he was going to say.

"The word just came down," Frank said, out of breath. "The North has won, and the South must abolish slavery."

"What?" Richard cried out. "It doesn't matter."

"I will never agree to free my slaves. Don't tell them," Robert said without blinking. "Let's try to get as much work out of them as possible. The North may have won, but these slaves are mine. I paid for them."

In the weeks that followed the end of slavery, there was panic and turmoil. Some slave owners went along with the law and freed their slaves. Many others refused to change their way of life.

Grimly seated in her parlor, Celia called all her remaining slaves to her. As each one filed in, she stood before them.

"Is this everyone?" she asked, going down the row, looking each of them in the eye.

"Yes, Miss Celia," they all answered.

"As you may or may not know, the North has won the war. A big change is about to occur. Slavery is about to be outlawed. As a result, you are all free."

Several slaves looked at each other. Tessie nearly passed out.

"If you like, you may stay around and earn your keep working for the house," Celia continued. "But all of you are free."

"Begging your pardon, Miss," Mark asked. "We are free?"

"Oh, so that's it?" Eddy asked. "No sorry?"

"Sorry for what?" Celia asked, confused.

"I hate you!" Eddy screamed as she scampered forward. "I will never work for you again! You treat us bad. Are we not human? And now that we are free, we don't even get a sorry?" Eddy pulled at the back of her dress revealing her scars. Mark grabbed her and pulled her toward the door.

"I will say no such thing!"

"Look what you done to me!" Eddy cried out. "You want me to hide it and cover them up? Look at me! You hear me? God will punish you for what you've done! I hate you!"

Mark managed to pull her out of the room. Celia was stunned but not shamed.

A few moments later, dozens of slaves walked off the property. It was hard for some to understand exactly what freedom meant. It took a while for it to sink in. Others continued like slavery hadn't ended at all, waiting for the government to tell them personally to stop. Most slaves didn't know they were free; they kept on working.

When the Union soldiers moved into Black River Plantation, their bodies were illuminated by a large roaring fire in the background. The federal occupation had begun.

Long lines of slaves carrying an assortment of personal items walked along small dirt roads to destinations unknown. John and several other soldiers walked along the path toward them. John stopped Curry, one of the emancipated slaves. "What happened to the house?"

"That master was always bad to his slaves, beating them and all," Curry said. "When his day of reckoning came, they showed him the same mercy he showed them."

As Curry walked ahead, John felt uneasy about Ellie. As more former slaves walked past him, he searched their faces, looking for a familiar one. The world he knew had changed. As his unit headed toward the plantation he had escaped from, he hoped he would see Ellie again.

The unit walked over to the front door of one plantation house to announce slavery had ended. Several slaves walked out. Walking from plantation to plantation, John loved the look on the faces of the former slaves when they first learned they were free. Some would just get up and leave without saying a word. Others would pass out.

As John's unit finally approached the Sneely Plantation, John recognized certain areas of the grounds and became excited. But as they inched closer, they saw that nothing was left, aside from the charred remains of a building. Through the rubble, they see that several other buildings had been set ablaze and the gutted remains of the big house. John walked ahead of the unit toward the house, looking around, confused and dazed. Taking out the handkerchief his mother had given him, he placed it to his nose. Her scent was still as fresh as the day she had given it to him. He took off running for the house.

"Ellie! Ellie!" he screamed.

Making it to the big house, he collapsed before a mountain of ashes and brick. Tears poured down his face as Gary approached him.

"Looks like a battle was fought here," Gary said.

At that instant, John sensed something peculiar. In that moment, he understood. Dropping to one knee and listening, he heard the cold reality of what had happened like a soft whisper in his ear. He heard Ellie's voice.

"Can you hear me?" she asked. Their souls remained and couldn't leave this place.

Since the Sneelys had no intentions of freeing their slaves, they killed them. Those who revolted were rounded up and pushed inside a barn, where several others were already locked inside. Two overseers smashed oil lamps against the outer frames. Many of the caged prisoners tried to force their way out, but it was no use. As the smoke quickly thickened and screams quickly mounted, they suffocated slowly.

He looks over and imagines. "VISIONS OF SLAVE SHIP AS THE FIRES WAGES".

1700's Slave Ship Heading to America. The interior of the ship is dark, cold, cramped, and filthy. Several hundred slaves chained huddled and quiver in the shadows of its hull.

In the interior of the hull, every single corner of the ship is filled with Africans, struggling to breathe.

He imagines, the ship interior is silent and dimly lit. The silence is abruptly broken by the thundering roar of water, and screams of men, woman and children. The ship quickly beginning to fill the interior. Several of the slave's struggle with the water inside the ship, eventually drowning. This mirroring the suffocating men woman and children in barn's burning.

CHAPTER
EIGHTEEN

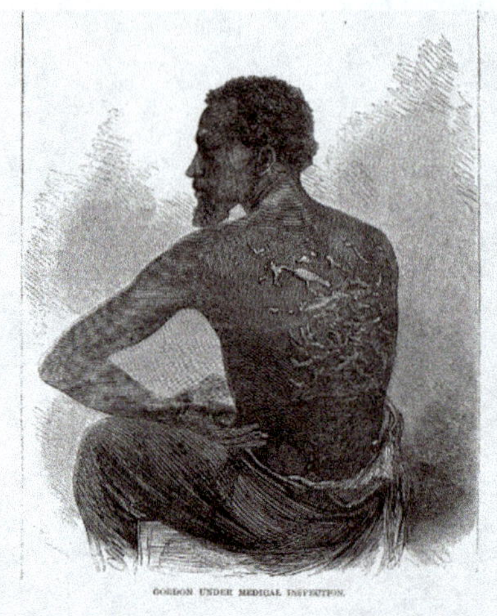

Chapter 18

Dedicated to Solomon Northup and the Black Union Army

1937

Langley was unsettled. John, sitting in a rocking chair, a pipe in his hand, took out a handkerchief and wiped his brow. Teary-eyed, he stared out into the field.

Langley leaned forward. "So they were murdered? All of them?"

John confirmed, pointing at the field. "Over there is what's left of Sneely Manor."

"How do you know?"

"They are here—all of them—burned alive in the barn over there. It's hard to describe. I hear it on the wind and feel it in my heart. I bought this little house to be near them. They will not rest until their story is heard. Come with me—I want to show you something."

"Where are we going?"

John stared at him.

"I know—less talking. I'm coming."

John walked Langley through the rubble, worn by the elements and time. A small section in the corner of the barn was not burned. Several chains were still present, and Langley dropped to his knees to examine them, badly mangled and sheered from the heat. "It shouldn't be possible," he said. "All of them killed, and all that's left are chains. The saddest thing is all of them born here, citizens of this country. All of them free when they were killed and never even knew it. What about you? What did you do?"

"Who? Me? We were left with nothing after slavery ended. Imagine working your whole life and having nothing to show for it. I didn't know what to do. I looked for my mother's grave. They didn't even give her a headstone. I loved music so much I became a musician, but I returned here to be close to Ellie. I rented until I had enough to buy this piece of property. Imagine that—from slave to property owner."

"It is some story."

John led Langley into the middle of a large field. "Pray with me. Close your eyes and open your heart."

Reluctantly, Langley closed his eyes. "What now?"

"Imagine millions of slaves, standing all around you. Each of them saying to you, 'Hear my story; feel my pain.' Make what they went through more than a ripple in the water."

Langley looked at John and smiled. "I believe you."

Back in New York, a month later, Langley stopped in front of his office building, noticing black people walking past him on the sidewalk.

"How far we have come." he said to himself before slowly making his way into the building. Two signs in his building's main lobby stopped him in his tracks. The one above a clean, freshly painted bathroom read Whites Only. A similarly designed sign above a dirty bathroom read Blacks Only.

He took the elevator to the fourth floor and knocked on his boss's door. Marshall Kelly swiveled around, seated behind a large and imposing desk. He motioned for Langley to come in.

"Have you gone over my report?" Langley asked.

"I read it—pretty detailed."

"What are we going to do about investigating his claims?"

"A slaughter of freed slaves in a barn—how do you know it's true? Did you get evidence to prove it? Did he see it happen?"

"No, but I have good reason to believe him."

"Surely you can see it won't hold up in a court of law. Almost fifty years after slavery ended, I was placed in charge of going over the mess it caused for this country. Hopefully there won't be any legal claims, and any claims will get absorbed by society."

"Sir?" Langley asked.

"My job has been to document, report, and verify claims made by former slaves. To tell you the truth, most people would like the whole thing to just go away."

"I understand. Maybe I can help?"

"You sure can. There are a couple more people we would like you to interview. Are you interested?

Langley nodded. Marshall handed him a folder. "Here is a list. You can get started on it right away."

"Why are we doing this?" Langley asked. "What is this going to do?"

"One of the greatest crimes in the history of this country was slavery. It led to a civil war—North and South being divided, a president assassinated," Marshall said, growing impassioned. "Brother fought brother, and millions died as slaves. Their stories and experiences all need to be documented by the government."

"But what will happen to their stories?"

"Realistically? Probably nothing. Who knows, but at least it will be recorded. Sometimes all you can do is just listen and record. No human tragedy should ever be forgotten."

Langley put on his hat. "I won't take up any more of your time." He collected a folder and walked out of the office. Rifling through the file of a woman, he wondered what her story would be. Marshall took John's folder and placed it in a file cabinet filled with numerous other cases. He filed John's name in alphabetical order and closed the cabinet.

The End

Middle Passage and slave port.

"Enslaved to Solider."

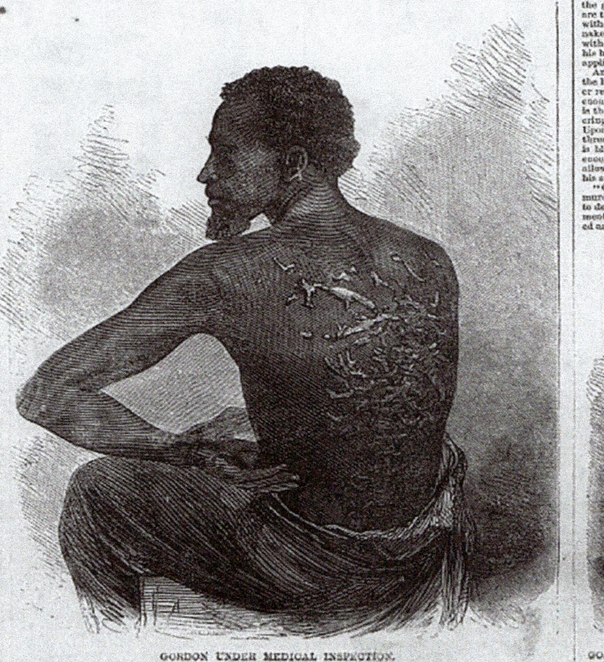

RAID OF SECOND SOUTH CAROLINA VOLUNTEERS (COL. MONTGOMERY) AMONG THE RICE PLANTATIONS ON THE COMBAHEE, S. C.—[SEE PAGE 427.]

[A TYPICAL NEGRO.]

WE publish herewith three portraits, from photographs by M'Pherson and Oliver, of the negro GORDON, who escaped from his master in Mississippi, and came into our lines at Baton Rouge in March last. One of these portraits represents the man as he entered our lines, with clothes torn and covered with mud and dirt from his long race through the swamps and bayous, chased as he had been for days and nights by his master with several neighbors and a pack of blood-hounds; another shows him as he underwent the surgical examination previous to being mustered into the service —his back furrowed and scarred with the traces of a whipping administered on Christmas-day last; and the third represents him in United States uniform, bearing the musket and prepared for duty.

This negro displayed unusual intelligence and energy. In order to foil the scent of the blood-hounds who were chasing him he took from his plantation onions, which he carried in his pockets. After crossing each creek or swamp he rubbed his body freely with these onions, and thus, no doubt, frequently threw the dogs off the scent.

At one time in Louisiana he served our troops as guide, and on one expedition was unfortunately taken prisoner by the rebels, who, infuriated beyond measure, tied him up and beat him, leaving him for dead. He came to life, however, and once more made his escape to our lines.

By way of illustrating the degree of brutality which slavery has developed among the whites in the section of country from which this negro came, we append the following extract from a letter in the New York Times, recounting what was told by the refugees from Mrs. GILLESPIE's estate on the Black River:

The treatment of the slaves, they say, has been growing worse and worse for the last six or seven years.

Flogging with a leather strap on the naked body is common; also, paddling the body with a hand-saw until the skin is a mass of blisters, and then breaking the blisters with the teeth of the saw. They have "very often" seen slaves stretched out upon the ground with hands and feet held down by fellow-slaves, or lashed to stakes driven into the ground for "burning." Handfuls of dry corn-husks are then lighted, and the burning embers are whipped off with a stick so as to fall in showers of live sparks upon the naked back. This is continued until the victim is covered with blisters. If in his writhings of torture the slave gets his hands free to brush off the fire, the burning brand is applied to them.

Another method of punishment, which is inflicted for the higher order of crimes, such as running away, or other refractory conduct, is to dig a hole in the ground large enough for the slave to squat or lie down in. The victim is then stripped naked and placed in the hole, and a covering or grating of green sticks is laid over the opening. Upon this a quick fire is built, and the live-embers sifted through upon the naked flesh of the slave, until his body is blistered and swollen almost to bursting. With just enough of life to enable him to crawl, the slave is then allowed to recover from his wounds if he can, or to end his sufferings by death.

"Charley Sloo" and "Overton," two hands, were both murdered by these cruel tortures. "Sloo" was whipped to death, dying under the infliction, or soon after punishment. "Overton" was laid naked upon his face and burned as above described, so that the cords of his legs and the

GORDON AS HE ENTERED OUR LINES.

GORDON UNDER MEDICAL INSPECTION.

GORDON IN HIS UNIFORM AS A U. S. SOLDIER.

INSPIRED
POETRY & ART
ABOUT
SLAVERY

INSPIRED ART WORKS ABOUT THE SLAVE NARRATIVES

Look Away, Run Away: A Son's Wish

Nightmares of a father, I hear the coming thunder and rain.

Lightning, look away, run away, Dad, they're coming again.

What's life if not the protection of pride, protecting your love ones while dying inside? Too selfless to die, you go on, existing in a never-ending cycle of a swan song. Dreams laid reefs over oceans, memorial to memories. The smile of a child, silent whispers of thoughts that ignite the pain. Look away, run away, Dad, they made you the enemy. Destiny's design is calling, you can't fight, get away. Me and Mom want to protect you—these bodies endure so much pain. I'll hold on to the memories, it's okay, run and never look back. Right now is forever, they will never matter, I believed in the light. The spark I saw reflected in your eyes, when you first smiled. It's locked away in the corners of our minds and lays in distant pride. Forever the moment beauty crossed our eyes, now forever beauty must hide. So special I had to look away, I knew you had to leave, the nightmare to begin. Taken with time violated in body, not mind, no sensibility to speak, heartlessly weep. That's okay, your strength runs through my veins, we run together in my mind, until heaven's gates. We are forever, here and now, it beckons me to endure, just a little while. Don't dare to dream. Days are not for wondering what could have been, or what could be. Our life is what it is, and it was never meant to be, I run to your arms, a constant promise of a mirage. I reach out my hand to touch your face, but your sprit is just outside my reach. They hate you and fear you, they see you and they want to lynch you. So strong the man, so deep the pain. I know how you feel. For me, with tears, look away, run away, live another day. I see in your eyes you know you can't fight these times. Under the weight of fear that will never go away. The lash on the back leaves lasting memory. Seeing others punished for your pride leaves you empty.

I hear it in your words, providence of the pieces of hope left to despair. Time is starting to erase it. You can't protect us from the path life has condemn us. Your presence too much to bear. I don't dare dream but live this nightmare and survive the long harsh days. Run away, try to live your dreams under stars free. Take away all the pain and this misery. Regrets will follow, but you won't see the tears, or the pain mommy feels. It's better to not have lost and cross oceans, the pain is much more than we can bear. Families, divided, under divinity's province. Sorry you were placed in this state. Look away, run away, Dad, my wish is that you escape. Look away, run away. Not to have to bear another day, entrenched in the echoes of the silent screams. Drenched in the thoughts of yesterday. Societies lash has no mercy. A backlash with fury. Our time is gone, there are no possibilities, mirrored against the resolve of the reality.

Lash after lash, whipped, I'll take it. Foot on my back, pull of the rope around my neck. I'll endure it. Move on, you can't save us. It pains me to say, what good's a day with you here? I will live for the days to see your face at that gate free from dark days like this. I would trade away the pain, not to live another day. You can't save mommy or me. Still, I wish the pain would end. Life is worthless, and I feel hopeless. Look away, run away, look away.

The Fight for a Life Worth Living

I pray life will give me the strength to show my son a life worth living. A place and time in the mind to wonder. Words that have meaning and purpose. Deeds and actions are worth more than to wish and wonder. Worldly, in a world seldom traveled, where life's mysteries are revealed.

Dreams are sometimes answered, prayers come true, divinity is seen in all you do. The vitality of life is echoed in every thought, passing glance, and each ideal. Take flight of fancy and prepare to land over oceans of opportunity. Rested under clouds of prosperity, nestled in the corners of the mind. Light shines through every door and the freedom of wonder is reflected and received. The fulfillment of accomplishment, satisfaction of sanity, and the rings bells of liberty. Free to think, wander, and feel whatever comes to mind. Courage and conviction to challenge those thoughts, to understand it meaning. A life free of distraction and filled with a sea of opportunity and revelation. As a mind can leisurely stroll through thoughts of possibilities, while reflecting on the inevitability of what will be. That a life that has traveled journeys in thoughts and prayers would lead to enrichment. Let light flood every corner of the heart and let the mind fill of thoughts that lift hearts. Freedom shadows, envelopes, all that flies under its wings. Uplifted under currents and pathways to peace, in a life worth living. You will never know how great you are, stardust. The thing of stars. Each forever a star formed from diamonds to rise in all its glory. Circle of light out of the disc of dust to transform. From the explosions of sound and light and waves and shades of color.

Each corner, a light shown reflects its true meaning. Illuminating darkness. Creating shadows of thoughts repeating. Steady state or forever expanding. Never to be another like you, to feel what you do. The complexity of the things you have seen. Perfectly human to a fault. To one day return and rejoin the stars. Rejoice in its majesty, from the state of being, state of living, with several tales to tell. To have dreamed the unimaginable or spoken the improbable and brought back thoughts to reality. There are no holes or doors in distant pass intersecting. Only a cross at the road for a fleeting moment. Through pathways, his story evolved into this story, which is forever history. The moment of thought is gone, forever a breath on the wind. Never a more perfect moment, never to see a more perfect world. Never to find that second time in a breath. Sleep on a bed of action, lay in the luxury of life's leap. At blinding speed, we are the ashes turned to dust to create the dream, from which glory rises from one day. When I imagine you. My hope is that you are not judged but loved.

Your mind wanders freely among the accomplishment you created. Wake up to the sunset in April, see a harvest moon, smell the jasmines in bloom. Only if that's what you want to do, you live your dreams, not what others plan for you. That you get a glimpse of your future, and safely navigate a course that takes you there. When I grow up, I want to be … all kids dream what they want to be. My only wish is you achieve. Remember all the hard work and the kind words. Feel the best times when it seemed the good times would never end. I wish for you a world where you can have all the tools you need. To build and devise the blueprint to achieve all you need.

That your efforts are rewarded. You believe long before you dream. Timely thoughts take you to where you are supposed to be. I will always imagine you, no matter what you do, living freely. To the fullest and till you are fulfilled, by a life created by you. Endowed by your endeavors and fueled by your efforts, the stuff dreams are made of. Drunk off life, high on living, hungover on memories. Of the days when you embraced your dream. That someone sees the content in your words and the value in your deeds. The character portrayed in every move you make. A life loved, forged on values you bring, and the way you choose to live. Footsteps walked, one man at a time, one foot at a time, it's your time to shine. Basked in warmth, breathe deeply on possibilities, dreams are the ally of brighter days. Relish, embrace, and love the man you will be one day.

Caged Bird Screams

God, I believe in you. Why do you forsake me? I pray every day and feel the lash at night. Do you hear me? What can I do to get your forgiveness? It's been twenty years enslaved to a system. In hell's garden every day. Tending to fields where dreams die. Picking cotton from sunrise to sunset. Until my fingers bleed, burned from the suns searing heat. My children punished for living. Can you have mercy on this tortured soul. Every day my eyes burn, mouth's dry, I feel nothing inside. Head hurts, body swollen from being smacked and beat. Bashed in the mouth for speaking. My body taken as property. Hated for breathing. What did I do to deserve this pain? Did I fail to pray or fall from heavens grace? Is my innocent child in hell to punish me? Do you need me to drop to my knees and beg for forgiveness? What more do you want from me? At night I can hear my own screams. I'm caged in body, while my mind flies free. I can see how life should be. Shade and clean clothes, nice things. A fan to bring cool air. Just a moment to daydream what life could be. Tea and honey on Sunday in my best clothing. Sitting in the shade with my family with Bible in hand. Then I'm awoken by my own screams. Realizing it was never to be. Tired and hungry, left starving. Food for thought, the cost is hunger and price is price.

No relief to speak of, the heat, no way to breathe, smacked when you learned I can write and read. Dreams do not visit here, where nightmares reside. Enemy of light, darkness's ally. I can hear the night cries of children I brought into this world, as they are beat mercilessly. Is that my crime, the children I brought here, I was taken, I did not want to give birth to his kids.

Nighttime drunken state, they took everything from me, with their sick twisted needs. Dogs are treated better than this black woman. At least they put them out of their misery. Do you think so low of me? That I should exist in eternal pain, damned to live a morbid reality? Married to pain, an existence below human. Air is horrible, food nauseating, life's unbearable.

At night no escape from the heat, the hunger, and I can hear the cries of other mothers. The men coming in the homes and the rape of women, explain to me why we go on suffering. I've seen the caged birds dream and scream in their nightmares and wake up in a worse hell. Night-scream screech, they come get me, beat me, throw me in a box to spend days in heat.

So much beauty, buried under scars of deceit, that reek of a relic from passages buried deep. Am I human or a sick man's property, am I the righteous or someone's thing to play with? I was born a mother, and watched them buy me, examine me, and rip my child from me.

Hear his scream when I lay me down to sleep. I screamed to every angel, none could hear. Explain to me, it's hard to believe, that this is what you want, or would allow. I cried so loud, cries on deaf ears, my tears mixed with fear, while blood flowed down my face. Woke up chained to a fence like a pet, less than a dog, less than human is how they treat me. Scorched earth, the dying fields are where you put me, beat with a stick, left in the sun to bake. Bareback burns with the sting of the whip, constant hits that cut through skin and heal over again. Cursed with the body and strength of men, will is dead, but the heart's too strong to give in. I wish they'd hanged me, wish they'd kill me, I would celebrate the day I died and would fly far away from here. Hear that bird, see her cry, see that bird soar up so high in her mind's eye, no escape for me. As the bars of the cage hold down her own flight, knowing she's just waiting for the time to die. Suffer every day until death does its part. The last wish of the weary to be put out of misery.

She cries because, not blind, she knows where she is, what should be, what's being denied. In the sky, able to touch clouds, see distant sunrises, climb and soar high close to stars at night. It gives flight to what was promised and could have been, as a child looks in a mother's eyes. It gives rise to what was denied and condemned when he was ripped from her arms. The caged bird cries its song. Sings sad, slow, and long, no rest, no reprieve, no relief.

Promised if I prayed, you'd be there for me, knelt at the altar on bended knee begging for mercy. At last, no more could I bear to believe, I'm the outcast destined to live this hideous nightmare. Forced to go on, I hear that poor bird's call, told her to go on, move on. I wish she would let go.

No more believing here. Dreams die slow deaths in this place, the purgatory of broken wills. Time's grains flow slowly, like the sand of time flowing through a distorted, broken hourglass. Suffering every second, mourning every moment, remembering every day, the loss and pain.

My time seems to slow to a halt, a day seems like an eternity, a week another lifetime. I can still hear that damn caged bird's crying, its poor silent screams, shrieking its song to me, which are now the sounds I hear at night, of me crying out about this lost life.

The So-Called Good Old Days

The good old days were not good for all, where women could not vote, blacks could barely find work or receive equal pay, much less equality. Values were not valuable. Equality, one need not apply. Unless the employer was blind. The truth sightless to the inconvenience of your need to survive. Preapproval was not happening, delivery not accepted, no acknowledgment given, return to sender. No eating at countertops or drinking at water fountains. Labeled colors for drinking, not colorful in thinking. The signs were all over, instead of red, white, and blue, signs bleached red with blood, stating whites only. Bleeding out all the rainbow of colors, the full spectrum. What should have applied to the law of the land? What did apply, the perverse distortion of ignorance? Everyone should be equal, a constitutional contract won with blood, sweat, and tears. Then violated by inaction. A life worth living, having a job where you can provide for your family. Having time to spend, and the energy to reap life's full bounty. To live a healthy productive life. A life worth living. Too many live a life of uncertainty, despair. One where instead of living, they are dying a slow death. A perpetual fight to the death, but I will not throw rocks at tanks. What does it do, what does it prove? I'll throw thoughts into the wind and see where they land. Gone but not forgotten are the days that brought hope, of the coming sun. Its warmth, its embrace, the feeling anything was possible.

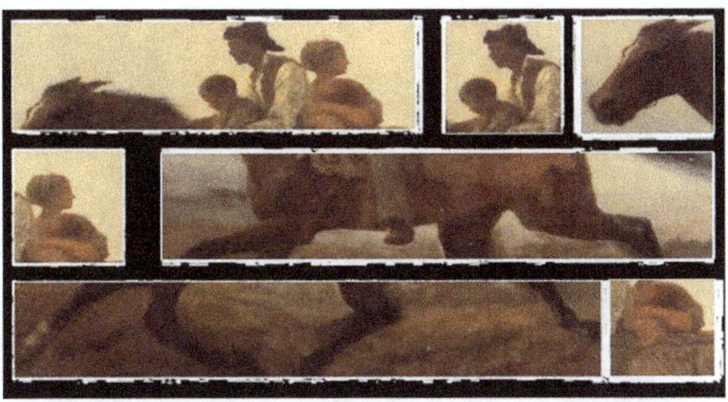

How Little Has Changed

Told to make way for change that's incomplete. Down on knees in prayer, why can't I be all I can be? From dusk to dawn I hear it calling us, why fight another day? Four hundred years, still a slave to injustice and inequality. Every breath a remembered feeling, deep breaths fill the lungs with pain. We still here. To face the pain. To give all, for what, just another day? It means more than that to me. Our position is to bear witness to the inscriptions. Paradise lost, this isn't, nothing's changed, time marched on, seats just rearranged. Why march, I continue to pray. Thinking to the Lord how little has changed. Taught free speech, but it ain't free when it can cost you your job, your life, and sanity. So it was written, had to hide the fact I could read or be right. Because knowledge scares the weak minds. If you're black, there's no such thing as free speech, when everything has a consequence. So my hands tend to the land. My tongue silenced. When I pray, I wonder how will he hear me? Just to spite, I can't show I can write. My words flow out like the sea to shores, brings waves in. Try to fill voids, look up to the sky and try to find dignity's eye. Sunrise, its love before the rise, and hate after the fall. Enveloped in the darkness. I simply ask why, why be born to endure such pain, carry such a heavy load, again and again. Embraced my Bible, the world's words' riddles, keep my mind occupied, my only salvation. Searched it every day, what section covers this type of suffering, the relief of a new day. From cover to cover, you search but find no answers. Buried deep inside hope for the past. Maybe there is no answer, the book just gets you through your day. Helps you find a way. I refuse to believe, when so many before me believed salvation was just a little way away. Like them, I search to find the way, and think to myself, how we repeat yesterday. How little has changed.

Bittersweet

Almost there is bittersweet. Little progress halfway is not the right way. Glass not half full, it's totally empty. Sold a dream, a lie in waiting, not to be believed. Half a man, half the pay, treated like half a person, given half the vote to play with. Told to control those looks. Keep my tongue in check. I thought we had free speech. I see the promise of a free society, hypocrisy, and how it's denied to people of color. Black and brown men and women treated like second-class citizens, get evicted. How the margin for error is zero and their power is unwelcomed, struggling just to get by. For some, every day brings the same experience. Why can't we make it in the land of promise? They say, you're not welcome, this is not your home. Go away. No work here. Treating you as if you're some sort of deprived stepchild. You can look at the table but can't get the scraps. You can look, but don't touch. You will never get a seat at the table. You can spend your money, but not bask in liberty's glory. Sad thing about Rosa Parks against the bus company. The buses were all supported by black people. We paid for the privilege every day, to be discriminated against. Didn't occur they treated their customer, like second class citizens. When they paid the bill. Boycott didn't change minds, it hurt pockets and profits. Which will cause change quicker than anything. When customers or sponsors stop paying, suddenly everything changes. Think about the areas where it doesn't involve money, the criminal justice system. Think how young black males feel, on a one-way path to poverty, a journey to jail. Police Stations dropped on top of his head. We worry as a son of a father, and a dad to a son, what his future will be, will he succeed? How many unarmed black young men have to get shot? As a Christian black father I thought we were a community of peace. Our country as a nation of pride, has solved so many things. Is there a will, a willingness to challenge things? Or be forever bittersweet? Given this beautiful tree of life and liberty but denied the fruits that hang from it.

CREATIVE
ART GALLERY
INSPIRING
POETRY

Icarus's Flight of Life

Reach high, try to touch the stars, if you fall you reached the apex of life. Look into the eyes of life, the face of God, soar higher in the mind than any others before. On the quest for excellence, to be the best, born with the tools to uplift. Spirituality tied to this place, soul's domain, prison of the physical, vice of the mental. The social gravity is so heavy, can't reach higher than you can think. Strive toward a force, fueled by dreams, deeply rooted and contagious, everything must balance. Be courageous, a spiritual bird in flight, in your mind's eye, that can soar above the clouds. Gifted and lifted, glide over warm currents of wisdom, leading to your salvation. Tides fueled by moonlit nights. Walk among the clouds, not satisfied, tried to touch the sky. If your goals are high, it can cause you to rise. You must push limits to the highest of heights. No time. Liftoff in anything will take most of your energy, one shot, and one chance to be free. Once airborne, you'll see the pressure, the strain, the push to get to heights never seen. The goal is to overcome, life's boundaries, restrictions on the body, God's design, man's blueprint. Life's desires hold you close to the vest, yet you struggle to get a lift, medieval is the design. They won't let you leave, hold you back with everything. Fill you with doubt and self-hate. A system pulling down shooting stars. You dodge so much just to get liftoff. In the air, all your energy expended, lost so much, the only thing left is to complete the task. You push to rise, push the limits of life, push what the mind, body, and soul can take. Deafeningly loud, blinding lights. Seems out of control, pass the point of no return. Heart overloaded, spirit trying to cope, thoughts provoked, despair, too strong to break. As you rise, what a spectacular sight, a meteoric rise in the night sky, for all to see. The Icarus dream blinded by envy. Reach high, like a moth to the flame, wings burned. We can't see the way we think, and the things we pursue are often relics from childhood. Higher and higher till there is no purpose, no rhyme for the rise, touch the face of the sun. Burn up in a blaze of glory's light. Glory, glory, and forget the wings that took us here. Damn their flaws, they can't take the heat. As the ascension becomes sacrificial. The godly act becomes a mortal defect, the light glow of the wings symbolizes the fall of man.

The sun's glow so overwhelming, couldn't let go, looking up as you fall, you know it's over. Succeed in scope, failed in reach.

When they preach, they will say Icarus never considered his wings burning or the fall from grace. Encroached on life's limits, a mistake to tempt the Lord's domain, trying to reach heaven's gates. As you continue to fall, return from where you come. You look up at the sun and notice it's just another star.

Ali Prize Fight

Fight of my life, I know I can out-think anyone, out-fight everyone.
Prime of my life, run circles around any challenger.
A times-bred warrior molded and cast out of plight.
The best of the best, in any context, there is no contest.
But the fix is in, enemies all around, I got no friends.
In shadows I see serpents, in hazes I can see the plan laid, the demise is imminent. Everything tonight is against me in this fight.
The ring is designed to catch and hold my feet
No matter, I will box with intellect and without moving.
A true Spartan who fights using tactics and technique.
Descendant fire burns throughout my veins, never uneasy.
He who wears the crown, bears witness, to its full weight.
The heart is greater, wade through the weeds, with kingdoms come challenges. Will you hide in darkness and in plain sight until the timing is right? The arena, the roar. The ropes of the ring grab and take hold. They wrap my hands and try to hold me back. Squeezing my lungs, suffocating me, till my last breath.
Wrap around my arms, and tightly around my neck.
They try to intentionally employ deception, misdirection, till I become my own enemy. I can't breathe, I can't breathe; No matter, I fight on. Life's warrior, descendant from kings, relinquish never. The odds stacked against me, I feel the buckle in the knees. Still I press on, sit high on Gibraltar's altar, heir to the throne.
It's not a game, many slain, I hear the roar of the crowd. The pull of those seeking the thorny crown. They slowly pull me down, while I battle to stay on top. Immobilized, engulfed in hostile seas of conviction and contention. Need to get closer to my foe, I sense their hesitation, designs on my annihilation. Too scared to look in my eyes, I'm too smart, I see the trap. You can't go toe to toe, you got a glass jaw. A victim of his own ambitions, I'm a one-punch Ryder, through my ambitions, tyrant. Sending one thought out, you can hold me, never will you ever control me. Got to get closer, all my training has taught. I'm right here. I showed up and got in close, waiting for the right moment. While leaning against its mass, I feel the chains and the weight. No fairness or honor, referee keeps on cheating, rules are stacked against me. No matter, he's lost and doesn't even know it, too quick to the hit. He's holding onto me, for dear life, the referee knows this bout is over. It's undeniable, I am unbreakable, it must be unfathomable, what you make of it. Without hesitation, I put my heart into one punch, connect, he falls. There is no one there to count him out, no one to see, and no one left to congratulate me. No roar of the crowd, just the throne, and a thorny crown.

Throw Up My Hands

Great Depression fighting getting depressed. Regression for my people. This ain't living. Food's gone, lights off, hope slipped out the back door. Trying to stay alive, plenty of drive, but no jobs, no way to survive. Promises not adding up, dollars made into cents, it all makes no sense. Roof blown off a tormented soul, fend for yourself, try to carry on. Gone are lazy days, now its dark days, survival is the name of the game. Great Depression is the doorway to despair. The breakdown of the family. Marvin Gaye said, "hands up," think about the children. He said hands up, makes you want to holler. Hands up in the air. I can't breathe. Employment none, opportunities gone, unarmed murders. Nightmares begun. They keep giving me the business, without paying for it. Lies, telling me things will get better. When we know they're not? The sun will come out, but never shine on this side. The sun will come out. Bet it don't shine on my side of the town, it always rains trickle-down economics. In an economic haze, starving becomes the craze, working for nothing is the new slavery. I got a tempest-brewing anger, a disbelief hangover, clouds storming, relief not coming. Fog settles in as I tiptoe through a path with thoughts that ring clear, are we less than human? Everything that's mine is a landmine. Survival's my only mission survives the new caste system. Put a sign on the border, cheap labor wanted. Leave the border open, who hired these workers? They are pathway dreamers, day-one believers, children born here to be second-class citizens. If they take a boat, they are immigrants, walk on land they are illegal, about fifteen million. This gives rise to the contradiction. Why invite the cheap labor without a plan to deal with it? Riling up the citizens, with distortions, when you purposely left the door open for cheap labor. Imported anger, deported dreams, robbed them, a mirage of prosperity, and gave them poverty. America is still the dream, better than any other place. I keep thinking, when will things change, throw up my hands Marvin said, "hands up," think about the children. He said hands up, makes you want to holler, "Hands up in the air. I can't breathe."

Incarcerated Kings

Incarcerated kings share fleeting moments on death's doorstep. Sworn enemies to the corruption of monarchy and sovereignty end. Reigns can't last forever, movements last an eternity. Battle is for supremacy and legacy. Wave the white flag, concepts in fatality, see the underlying symmetry. Helpless to fate, mental chains engaged, convictions rearranged. Distorted reality, the damage severe, and the plots clear. Flee, take the covenant and the altar, while the cups runneth over. Leave behind the sacrificial and the martyrs. There evolved many plots amidst relics and warrior envy. Rue the day etched in stone. Hear the calling, the revenge for the fallen. Quest to direct is kept secret, breakout enviable of the wrecked. Plan to elevate, methods not to alleviate, counter to evade the demise of the protectors of faith. Win by any means necessary. Broken thrones, crowns gone, robes burned, and Kingdom come. Buried deep, enshrined the treasure of the shroud. The refusal for a lie to stand the test of time. Not for long, eyes wide with fury, fires burn, while they're locked in envy. Jealousy can't envision the duration or campaign and the march to victory. The third eye jurisdiction and justification. Thirteen cloaked kings, burned at the stake, forever words rise from the flames. Birth to the grave, can't hide from destiny, what you did, or from the enemy from within. Warrior's words creep silently, as soldiers come for vengeance. Battle cries to the masses linger on for an eternity. Erratic the times, distracted lines, break the shackles, did you reach America? What was once will be again. Escape to wrestle with giants, survive the empire, the king avenged. Long live the protector. Overthrown, the resurrection vindicated by history, and the formerly incarcerated king. Sun at morning glows and the night recesses in the mind. Soothing, enveloping all with its protection. Dawn's light is the transition from darkness, the sunset is the transition to enlightenment. Colors fold into darkness to bring forth the light, it is the messenger of good things to come. It isn't the absence of light, it is the stage from which light can be brilliant in all its glory. Light can take center stage; the darkness is its humble companion. Offering encouraging words, inviting sounds and rest to the weary. Darkness is the prelude to all good things to come.

MADIBA NELSON MANDELA

Touched the hand of a dream, seen a smile on his face.

Heard the words of the King Nelson Mandela, Madiba.

He spoke to me with a smile on his face. His life's work says fight on for what you believe. Words could never do justice to the spirit you feel, the highest level of respect you could reach. Shackled in body, free of mind, kindhearted, lionhearted, a kindred spirit to mankind.

Where men have fallen, he stood tall for the beliefs of what it is to be free. Never faltered, never caved, and gave it all. One of the greatest of warriors we've known. So much the king conqueror, bearer of that which is good in humanity and all of us. Through your grace, you improve the state of the human race. A chance to be unified in the struggle, you gave them the beacon of light to follow. Societies smile, a compassionate kiss, a gift to the world, the embrace of reason. Glory, the sun, our star, nurtured your rise, legacy's light guides all you've done. A mind clear, heart pure, came through the darkest tunnel to the other side, Bells ring, angels sing, rejoice the glory, of one of our great kings. Roots grow strong and deep, they cling to the motherland, the foundation of life. Anchored to her, she's the creator and protector. A land that gave strength to a legend, the legend built a shared legacy. For such a deeply rooted person, the struggle never ends. To be righteous in life you must struggle and fight for those less fortunate. The joy of life, lives in support of freedom's clemency. To have lived so long deprived, for what you believe. Suffered injustice at the hand of another.

Offered the hands of mercy and lenience, as forgiveness is what you preach. Kissed the hands of those locked in life's injustice, who yearn to be free. You moved on to the greater, you stood strong for a nation. The creator sent an angel to lead humanity's calls. Forever will be the spirit and body of Africa. From Apartheid to it's our time, guide the hands of the giant. The sunrise, father of a nation, civil society's hopes and aspirations. From bended knees to ancestry's dreams. Opened a window for all to see. The world is blessed to have had a moment to shine in your historic rise.

Life on the Run

Enslaved to live a life on the run, denied prosperity and progress. You're the present, forever in spirit. As our clashes with the past enter our present existence. To live at your side is worth the pain, from the rib we share, until we are whole again. The visions of you and me against the world. Warriors fighting a war. A battle they say cannot be won. No mercy, bodies locked as one, embraced forever in our word. We need justice, everything right in keeping all safe. Worlds away, from where we want to be. Inherit the progress, my ride or die, never falter if they try to break us, think Gibraltar. The rock is forever, an oasis to Ossie Davis, and Ruby Dee, or Camille Cosby, the feelings run deep. Starlight, star bright, at night, you're the brightest star in sight. Wishing on you to deliver me, rescue me, come save the humanity you know that's deep inside of me. Locked in storm's sight, you know that's where my eyes are locked. The center of the storm, the calm before all, the coming that was foretold. Where the heart is, they can burn down the house around us. Your embrace, saving grace, that can take me far from this place. Crosses burned in yards, ropes hung from high, dragged down dusty roads, no tears, it doesn't matter, the only image is that of your smile. Can't take away our embrace, these moments we celebrate, in God we trust, in body we suffer. You delivered me to this place, give me the strength to find another way to live another day. The struggle is sinister, the hustle is hell, Harlem forever, and it's all unreal. Each blow is my blow, each cut is my cut, your hurt is my cross, your pain is my agony, in your life I rejoice. Can't take my joy buried way deep. But we don't break, we grow strong, our love lasts longer. Coretta Scott to King or Betty Shabazz to Malcolm X. The struggle runs deep, bodies bear the scars, burn crosses on the lawn, burn houses down. Shot both of them, dead, on the mountaintop we sit. Ride or die till time claims our bodies. Minds linger on, legacy forever lives on. A life mixed of love and fury at a system trying to defeat us. No matter, no way can they destroy what we have. The Passion, the visions, give grace to look into your eyes to see that happy face. Take my hand, this moment is ours for an eternity.

A Moment of Silence

The collective conscious bears the scars of the pain we survived. Too scared to hope, too much fear to deny. They really do come true, it can happen to you. The heart was once young, that beats inside of you. Too wise to think it would come to this. Someday my nightmare will die a slow death. Married to that day when it would all come to an end? Tired of burning crosses, deaths in churches, lynching, hangings, and enemy flags. Is it In God We Trust, Don't Tread on Us, religion versus a historic bloodlust? Share the lessons of life, or swear on a stack of Bibles, worship our flag. Or too scared they despair, cling to all they hold dear? Believe our worst fears? In faith we stand united. In race we are still divided? Promote unfairness and narrow minds. A moment of silence for the fallen.

We screamed death to intolerance, and death to no progress.

Then another moment of silence. Did they hear our prayers?

We need a moment of silence for the one-sided dearly departed.

On this day Racism died a tragic death, survived by its only child Prejudice. Today we lost Ignorance, such a tragedy, committed suicide, a shot to the head. Bigotry died of a heart attack, an unhealthy heart, caring is what it always lacked. Blood disease through history, hate-tainted pathogens clogged its arteries. Seized up, engorging itself on a powerful cocktail of ego, fear, and self-hate. Prejudice went quietly into the night. Died in a retirement home, where old thoughts go. Sexism died, may she rest in peace, died driving recklessly, off a cliff in a blaze of glory. In our community injustice died so suddenly. In a mental ward for the criminally insane. Twenty-one-gun salute, jets fly, "Taps" plays, salute raising the flag, salute our calling. Salute all the fallen. May they live as historic reminders? May they receive the highest civilian honor? Enlightened we stand in honor, in darkness we fail in common? A nation, seen in full color, so vibrant are the colors when they are next to each other. Let's say a couple of words for the fallen and put an end to the violence of dividing. It's been long overdue, let's have a moment of silence for our so dearly departed.

Victim No More

I used to dream, fly high with possibilities, on beautiful wings I built from experience. But now I "forget you," for what you do, but I can't ever forgive what you did to me. You've given me worry and pain so you're not worthy of my prayers or forgiveness. I'll never care about you, I am not a liar, not going to fool myself, don't believe it. Don't wish you joy, or care about your pain, you are empty to me, not worthy to breathe. What you did to me. It's easy to see. I will never be the person I was meant to be. What should I do, be angry at you? Give you another victory over me? Let you enter my head, like you entered my life and took from me the light? What was promised to me was a life; living is now trying to survive another day. Is it so much pain you had run through your veins? In a rage, you injected your hate into me. Or was life so unkind, you couldn't find the time to show compassion for another? In an instant you took from me what was hidden. Now I live the life of a victim. Nightmare-daydream, bear witness to me held down, taken while my soul tried to escape. Out of body experience, floated over my body and looked back for a second, to see the tears. Tried to fly away. Didn't want to witness my life's destruction. Shattered and broken to pieces. Fly away is all I could think. As high as I can, soared pass the trees, to the heavens, on to the sun. Reached high to the sky, thought I left it all behind, hide the pain, mask the scars, try to let it go. The heat of the sun, trying to go numb, dilemma of Icarus, the blinding sun burned off my wings. The fall of an angel, with chains and weights. Came crashing down to earth never to fly again. When I returned at night, to visit what was left of my body. I cried for her, fully knowing what she just lost. Insanity fights it, memories deny it. Absent was the light that used to beat close to my heart. My mind in a haze, heart in a rage. I gather my tattered body, try to wash away the pain and scrub away what was done to me. There are not enough tears to cleanse the body, mind remembers, heart records, soul witnesses. Mind understands things will never be the same, the thoughts keeps flashing in my head.

Victim No More II

Echoes of screams I can still hear. The taste of blood mixed with tears. Permanent tattoos of anger etched in my soul. Body branded forever yours. You took from me all I hold dear, you gave me the nightmare that seems to never end. Thrown into darkness, a sunless world. I see a light in the distance, I keep chasing after. The closer I get to it the farther it disappears. Chasing the next light on the highway of life. In those dark places, well contained. Down the well in a pit of hell, made to hold beautiful souls. My mind's eye can't soar, my wings long gone, the love in my heart tries to linger on. I can see the distant light at the top of the well. Flooded with tears of despair, the deeper it gets. Each foot I climb I slip back down. In darkness, try to focus on one step at a time. "Time heals wounds" is nonsense. Not the regrets or memories of what has been taken from me. Can't shake the memories and false dreams, of one day being free of all of it. Time has locked me in a place, a space from which there is no escape. I do the work, I did the math, and know how hard it is to nurture my body back. I'm sad for my heart and soul, they are like two innocent kids that witnessed it all. Changed forever, neither will ever be the same, they never talk about what they saw or the pain. Know it will never be what it once was. Their tears hide the depth of the pain they feel. Warrior wounds heal slowly. Thoughts of what they endure never leave. Pain forever lingers. I wonder what life would have been, if you would have never forced me to endure your pain. Carry your luggage, take on your struggle. Behold pain, I'm your greatest creation. Rape of the innocent. Murder of dreams and the destruction inside another human being. I try to forgive and forget, but for what? I'm barely living. I'm supposed to be drifting on soft shores of possibility. Barefoot, walking on sunshine. Instead, I'm distressed, trapped on a sinking ship in the ocean. Waiting for help that can't find me. Can't say I forgive you, that would be a lie. Or that I want you to suffer, sink to your level. Can't say I wish you the peace you denied me. I don't feel that in my heart it's the right move for me. My struggles are very clear to me. My mind wishes to be free of the poison pill you gave me. So I can't forgive you, so forget you! For the life that could have been.

Post-Racial Hangover

Post-racial hangover. Still no progress. Post-racial is the goal, we still haven't solved. We hold these truths to be evident, that we are not equal. We are a nation divided, along economic and power lines.

Race relations are about economic empowerment, tolerance, and social change. We elected a black president and thought we were on our way. To a better day, to balance out liberty's reign.

Things come to the surface, nothing is done. I wonder if it were someone else, would we be better off? How do we give promises to immigrants, migrants, the dreamers, and nonbelievers?

It's hard when everything is designed to divide the people.

We were called black, because skin color divided us.

Made it easy to own another human being or discriminate. They are not like you and me. Slavery, an injustice whose hand touches today.

Labeled black made others believe, it's okay to deprive. Even Christians in the Bible. That it's not a sin to own another human being. Stolen, bought, sold, treated less than human. You have to know your history if you want to fix it. No education, no salvation, told not to write or read, less than human. You can tell something is wrong, when a term is used to divide us. When every other culture is named after the country it comes from. Germans from Germany; Italians, Italy; French, France; Russians, Russia. Show me on a map the country that's called white or black. Its name is America, the root of the problem is dividing people in camps, so the rich benefit.

Keeping the poor and middle class going at it each other.

While someone at the top is benefiting from it. This generation has a chance to succeed and hopes they do better than we did.

The need to address the social ills that plague society.

Must start with a history lesson and some deep reflecting.

You must know where you come from to know where you're heading. Open dialogue with sincere and reasonable people.

Maya Angeluo

Starlight shines a happy cry, for an eternity.

Long walks along life's orchids, left words of encouragement.

The last line of the song "Loving You" is "Maya," fitting. It's easy to see, because you're an angel. Maya's song beams words into melody's memory.

She, a brilliant light illuminated in the spirit of the spoken word.

Forever rise, a phenomenal woman, pulse of the morning, heart of a woman.

And still I rise, Jalen, a spiritual melody, mystical bird, take flight Maya, an angel's special light. Visit distant worlds, dream words in pearls, jewels left to glisten. Nuggets left to interpret. Diamond-lined caverns illuminate every dark space of the race to be human again. Live high on seas' shores, walking in His footsteps, of phrases, words mixed with thoughts. Carried in the thought of not what will be, but what was. The brave and the bold.

God on high spoke life through her eyes. Life's pen bears witness, mightier than any voices. Seen words in other worlds fly through clouds colorful. Moved by will, enlightened by pain. Fingertips left their impressions on faces of all touched. Words lingering in thoughts. That cage still sings, knowingly embraces, the power of words forever unyielding. Without a breath, made a breach through walls and long-fought wars. Left passages so deep scholars still search for meaning. Buried treasure in poems written.

Tantalizing as it is, buried deep, the treasure far-reaching. That summer breeze fanned on a porch with sugar-honey iced tea. A fan, the fields, the sun's heat, shade from clouds, the wind's gentle kiss. A smile on my face. A mind racing with dreams, words jump from heart to pen to paper. Write in seclusion, give birth to life. To think, if only life could freeze in that moment in time. When your mind's eye journeyed over liquid vanilla skies.

So much to do, so little time to say, the voyage of enlightenment just beginning. You pushed the power of the possible, probable, and created the unimaginable. A sighting of brilliance caught drifting out to seas.

Quick-witted, able to see the big, it was all a dream. Harlem's light rests with the best. A light through words and eternity of rest.

Not My Problem

It's always the pride before the fall. Because it's not your kid you do nothing at all? Not your wife no need to worry, all I hold dear is safe.

Men lie, women lie, while kids die, what's your reply? Nothing? Let them starve on despair. Feed on anger, washed down with rage. What about community, the air we all breathe? The judgment of time, what about life's legacy? One day you'll stand before the face, feel the wrath, and know your fate. Judgment for all, for what you could have done. Standing on the sidelines means you cosigned the demise. Think once, it was you. How often we forget. The hit of the fist inflicts pain on your family. Just another woman and more children crying in pain. Screaming and yelling from upstairs, it's not in your home. You don't care. You feel you can look away. Concerned only with your own. Heard the taking of innocence, you didn't shed a tear. Hugged your own child, turned up the music, and wished it all away. The rip off of clothes, loud screams, you don't care, act like you can't hear. It's not your cherished souls, so you let go. Did you forget the gift you received of a blessing everyday? The promise with every beat to protect your hearts. Karma's crazy like Cosby. In life you give, so those you love can receive. Hope you shield their days, they walk freely, never forget, the sin gets passed down to them. Is it so long ago you forgot, where you used to be? On bended knee, dreaming of life, or fighting for your life on knees in prayer. Distant are the thoughts that weigh heavily on the past. Proud is the day victory reigns. You fought all foes and defeated all adversaries. To arms, to arms; someone came to your side. Reverence on high, right on your side. The promises of peace came to the side of the righteous. Morality has its cost, not the Trojan but the dark horse. A victim anywhere is a victim right here. Blessing on high, the tool to defeat all. To prevent life's suicide get involved. There is no valor in looking the other way.

JACKIE ROBINSON, SWEET SWING

Jackie Robinson, sweet swing, only if they let us in.
We could do anything if they let us win.
We could be anything if they let us prepare.
Not trying to walk on water, just do our thing.
Let's walk up to the gates of power, with a confident stroll.
Knock on the gates, open the door, so we can see who's home.
Will they let us in, or abandon everything, scream "leave us alone"?
We ain't scared no more, are they running scared, because we found out they're weak? Scared of losing their place, if we could be all we could be?
Competition, the last thing on their mind, hold onto power till they die.
Power to the people if powers not shared. Tear it down, break it up. No monopoly.
They're playing with fake money, but we came prepared, to give it all we can.
The door swung shut, they locked the door, window closed, and they pulled the curtains down. No shades on our sight, or wool over the eye, no more shades and blinder time. See evil, speak evil, and no more depriving the dreams of the people.
No one's home, they act like they're not one of us.
You feed and bleed, you're just greedy.
What could it be if they let us in? We could all be winning.
Jackie Robinson, sweet swing, if they let us in.
We could do anything if they let us win.
We could be anything if they let us prepare.
All we need is a seat, be it on the bus or at the table.
They are in a privileged position without the deeper understanding.
Share the wealthy, we all benefit, let talent win over ignorance.
What's the difference between right and wrong?
The intimate burning desire for truth, not privilege that's flawed.
To deny is to be unworthy of the air you breathe.
Unworthy to be part of our humanity.
Court of public opinion, you're holding back progress.
The verdict is in, let them be all they can be.

War on Women

You declared war on women, why do you hate them so?
In the image of your wife, mother, or daughter.
Mother made us, mother may I, the passages to progress.
Why take from someone who gave you the gift of life?

The eve of sunrise, coming of a new day. They created the world, made you a man. To the rib gave you a shot, and the strength to take on anything. Daughters, the apple of our eyes, not an apple fallen to the ground and kicked. From the womb, strives stories, some of the greatest thoughts. In the tomb, encasing girls' ability to rise above all. Susan B. saved them, Harriet led them, Rosa took a stance, Stanton voted Kelly embraced them, Charlotte wallpaper, Jane Addams Hull House. Ida B. Wells anti-lynching, Keller connection, Hamer, Baker too strong to mention. Too much strength to act like you can't see what they accomplished, what some could be. You wouldn't hold your mother back when she strived to give you everything.

You wouldn't hold your daughter back, you want her to live her life and dream big. Isn't she supposed to survive to make her way in the world? How can she make a living making half as much? Physically you feel superior, but can't no man survive pregnancy. Mentally you think you're smarter, when your ego is lying to you. Spiritually you feel God's given you everything. When a woman is at the core of the gifts you receive. Family is everything, do weak men rule the world? Why not make it a level playing field for all? I rise with my own hands, fall on my own. I never felt the need to put someone else down. My rise, feel like a man and free the women, let them earn, work, and grow. Open the doors. Welcome all challengers, relish at competing in life's arena. I've seen too many women, hearts pure, sprits bruised, left confused. Wondering how could love could cause so many wounds, abused dealing with the repercussions of events long gone. Heard too many stories of women pushed down, held down, never to get back up. In order to please the ego of a coward. I was raised you only put your hand on another man. Someone that can give you that true test, of man to man. But how do we define womanhood when you see it everyplace. Don't judge women, tough choices, who made decisions for themselves. Judge the men that want to make the decisions for them. Free the life-giver, the center of the family, the way to the light. Free old ways from a new enlightened society. Never put your hand on a woman or in her pocket.

Let's work together to end the war on women.

Celebrate You

Let's celebrate womanhood today.
From lover, to wife, to mother of the land.
Our lovers create the spark that lives forever and a day.
Our daughters are the ones we look to, to always please.
Wives are the light that ignited the spirit for the family.
Grandma passes down so much wisdom, from better days.
Gives the foundation for the family to grow stronger every day.
I thank Ms. Juanita, Ms. Ruth for the lessons they gave me.
Those days lying in your arms, frozen in that moment I wished would never end.
When a smile could melt the heart and words could get me back on track.
Better half, smarter than that, they are the reason we grow every day.
You are so blessed to find another who can fill up our life, complete every day.
Words can't state a soulmate, to grow young in mind, while wise in the body.
Give your heart freely, when you see what comes from a woman.
First child, you're alive, can't think of a better day.
That other half of a thought, other half of a child born.
Be the support, when I'm kneeling.
Give me the sense that everything will be alright, continue the fight.
So many shades, I don't know where to start.
All the way from light to dark, I love them all.
All the way from strong to in need, the strength of vulnerability.
So precious is the one that we cherish, wake up next to.
Every success we can go back and find there was a woman there.
Pushing her family forward, fighting to find a better way.
The backbone, and holder of the throne.
In so many shades, each color equally beautiful, each life equally brilliant.
Rainbow of life, a sunset walking on eternity's arms.
No matter what anyone says, womanhood has always been strong.
It's the eyes and smile, letting you know the wisdom they have.
Never take a backseat and keep pushing forward.
Too many women forget they could never judge or define you.
You do as you feel is the best for this moment.
Life goals and forked roads lead to wherever you go.
Sacrifice the dreams so the family could live.
This is dedicated to you. The life that, in my veins, came from your hands.
Dedicated to you, the dreams I feel are inspired by you.
Dedicated to you, all the hope my child could ever feel.
Dedicated to you, let's celebrate the women we love.

Bravest of All

Freedom's reign, the bravest of all, king-conqueror of darkness. Builder of great walls. Out of ashes rises. Sun-smiled skies. Stars and stripes forever, bound together. From stone to walls, to cracked throne and hollow crowns. The battle for freedom was waged and won. Be it ever so blessed, we are humbled at the majesty of our democracy. Nestled and protected between the grips of oceans, centered between them. God's favorite child need you forget your path, freedom to worship is how we landed here. What Kane struck, erupts humanity's deed, a blood-brother's bond? Blessed be the country that puts rights above all. Country first, spirituality above all.

Save yourself or the rest? Are they enlightened to see, broad enough to be saved? Willing to embrace promises of peace, or forever hold and release? Never have to grieve, for one world our world, the sun will never set on freedom's reign.

The Day the Skies Cried

Did it rain, I can feel the pain, see the coming storm
The tears run down in streams. Thunder, I could hear the screams. Blinded by the light, as the rain falls, the skies get cloudy, wind blows. Action is my vision, enacting doubt without despair, I can hear. I stand in judgment, can't think straight, but feel just like pain. As tears hit the ground, it cries up to me. The very ground I stand on, with its tragedy.

As time marches, decades pass, youth wasted on the young's thoughts. Hiding in each corner of the mind, locked away where only I can find. Hidden, the pain and suffering of what could be, and once was. Only if I still believe in the possibilities, or if it was not in doubt. From wind comes the force, to face off what will come. One blow can strike down two towers, the hopes of humanity. If one man is captive, we all are enslaved.

Humanity or Human-Unity?

Humanity without humility lacks the ability to hear or fear. Our strength in human-unity, desires outweigh ingenuity. Do we act when absolutely necessary, or before it's too late? Are we filled with kind words but not in-kind actions? Thoughts we breathe deeply on the winds of freedom. What of the thoughts of what could be, and what we are losing? I run free, feeling alive. Am I waiting to die or dying to live? Time moves fast or stands perfectly still. Seeds of dust and despair flow evenly. The ground screams out loud, I can barely think. Fears never subside, a fight to stay sanely alive. So many walked the roads seldom talked.

The injustice of an act can scream from above and below.

The memories of an experience yell from the wounds inflicted on a soul. With each passing tide comes the rise.

We all shed tears, for what is left by the injustice of an act.

Darkest before Dawn

We fought to see the unity. Eagles fly high. Stars and stripes forever soar in the sky. The dawn of a new time, the rise of the empire of life. Dreams of those that believe. Country of kings, versus the county of kings For queen and country is the call. Never retreat, fall back to live. Fight through the avenues of the city. Pass the African burial grounds to the cloisters on high. Defend the dream; nothing ventured, nothing gained. Never backing down, bow to no one. We are all kings in our own rights. Our father's song, liberty's call, to arms, we fight for all. Signs of the promise of tomorrow, from the nightmares of yesterday. The fall of darkness descends on the city, the rise of history's call. To arms, to arms, the bursting in air. From sea to sea, we are still here. The march to end all, the stars and stripes forever.

The taking of DC, the painting saved to survive the fall.

We fight for the rise of the empire of life, fall back, and fall back. Fight through Brooklyn, Manhattan, and the Bronx ,the fall of Staten Island. The red crimson waters flows, the stars block out the brightness of the sun. Journey through every corner. The Empire State stands tall. Benjamin's banter, Washington's gamble. The game is won.

Stand tall, never fall. The courage contested is won for all.

A View Fit for a King

My eyes have seen glory," he once said. Battle hymn of peace, a view fit for a king. Why we struggle, sometimes there's no right or wrong answer. Just a solution and resolution, and the words to influence it. What protection do we have from the coming storm? No food to eat, no shelter, no clothes that are warm. Try so hard to please but we get no respect. The greed that bites the hand that feeds you becomes the backbone of a movement. I was asked why fight when you know you can't win. I replied I'd rather die fighting a good fight. Than live avoiding it. I'll stand and fight on my feet until nothing's left. Not beg on my knees for mercy from them. I have seen both the best and worst in human beings. King's vision, poetic, prophetic. He's already celebrating with all humanity. Fragile is life, and time never waits I don't think I'll make it to the mountaintop. But the view from the valley below is extraordinary Looking up to all its majesty. Singing the battle hymn of peace.

Middle-Class Slavery

Harvest of souls, feast of families. As slaves they used to own us, now they rent us on the cheap. Harvest of Shame, the new slavery, where millions go back into the work fields, just like during slavery. Nothing's changed. Food's everywhere but none on the table for the working families. Not a harvest to mankind, or a harvest to the world, but a tragedy for the American dream. Wealthy starve democracy. Such a shame to live a life below minimum wage. In the last hundred years nothing's changed. It's the life of a slave, be it migrant workers or poor black folks from the South. Four hundred years, where's the respect for their efforts or progress made from their endeavors? People died in those fields, cheated out of money. So close to food but starving for respect, decent pay, and dignity. Can't get a decent night's sleep, body broken, after decades of nothing done. Recently, they've shined a light on some. But what happens with all of the other victims? Another tragedy of the harvest of shame, and what left is a debt for millennials legacy.

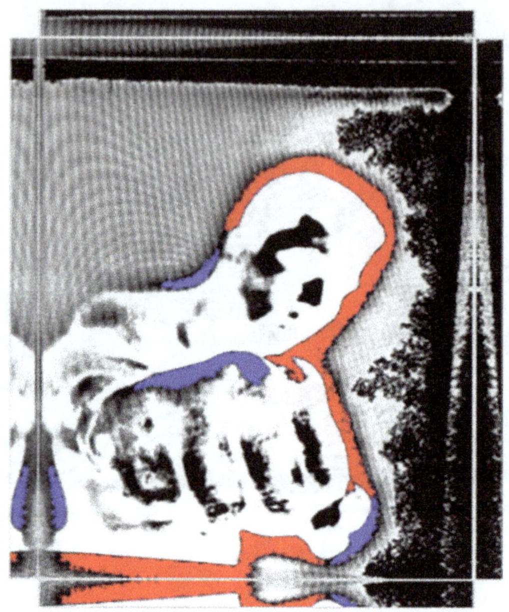

Life's Lashes

Man, woman, child, backbone to life. Stripped and parted. Taken away, the only reason worth living for. Left behind, the only thing worth dying for. Hearts bashed, under attack, seized, and under duress, mind filled with resolve. The salvation, the church, nothing can save but belief. Heartbroken, back broken, you get used to the lash of the whip. Tears shed, from the betrayal. With each blow, I get strong. Whips feel familiar. Each day in hell, one less day until death. The field is where I chose, the house is not for me. Every strike blinding like the sun, each moment a reminder of the blow. Tragedy of the spirit cuts deep, until I'm numb from feeling. The whip, I can feel the lash as it strikes. My back bare, but on my soul not a scratch, it has endured each lash. Mercilessly, without regard or regret. The lashes of life to test faith. It breaks trust and fills with false promises. I'm unbreakable, but the thoughts are unfathomable. I traveled the cold distant trials. I wonder how you can stand and judge when you look nothing like me, know nothing of me, but I'll take the lashes. My soul remains intact, your injustice is noted.

Sons and Daughters of Liberty

The ability to endure hundreds of years of slavery. Walk in glory sons and daughters of liberty. Dealt the harshest physical and mental conditions.

Survival and suffering, both uniquely intertwined. Survival constantly evolves.

There are levels suffering devolves down into unimaginable levels.

Families broken, rights violated, the depraved deaths of people of color.

What was true four hundred years ago is as clear today. I have inherited an enormous ability to endure. I think back to those who were enslaved. Without the brutal chains of injustice, they could have achieved anything.

It must have been painful to live under a flag of freedom and equality. But be denied its warm covering, betrayed by its song of freedom. Owning another human being. Could you endure living an existence less than human? A permanent underclass? Three-fifths a human to vote, why allow me to vote at all? Because of the possible political power of so many of us.

To be denied equal rights is to live a lie, and to die a slow painful death of liberty's cry. Today instead of three-fifths, mass incarceration has taken the vote and voice of millions away. We are still the sons and daughters of liberty, to see it so easily manipulated is hard to fathom. The hypocrisy of those who claim freedom's light but refuse to shine it in all corners of darkness. The core of greed is to self-feed and gorge themselves on selfishness. Power protects its power at any cost. The collateral damage, never acceptable, and justifiable.

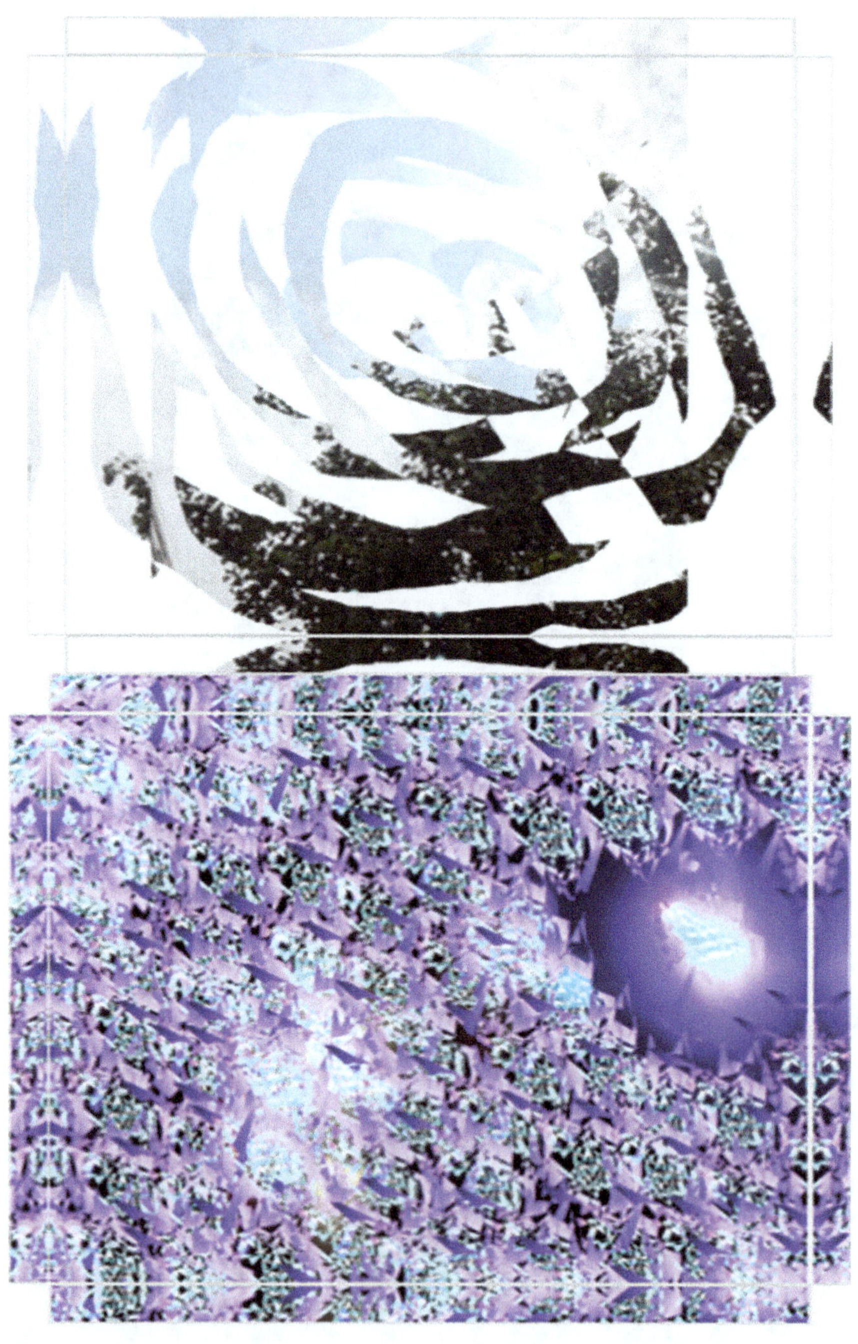

DELI FOOD

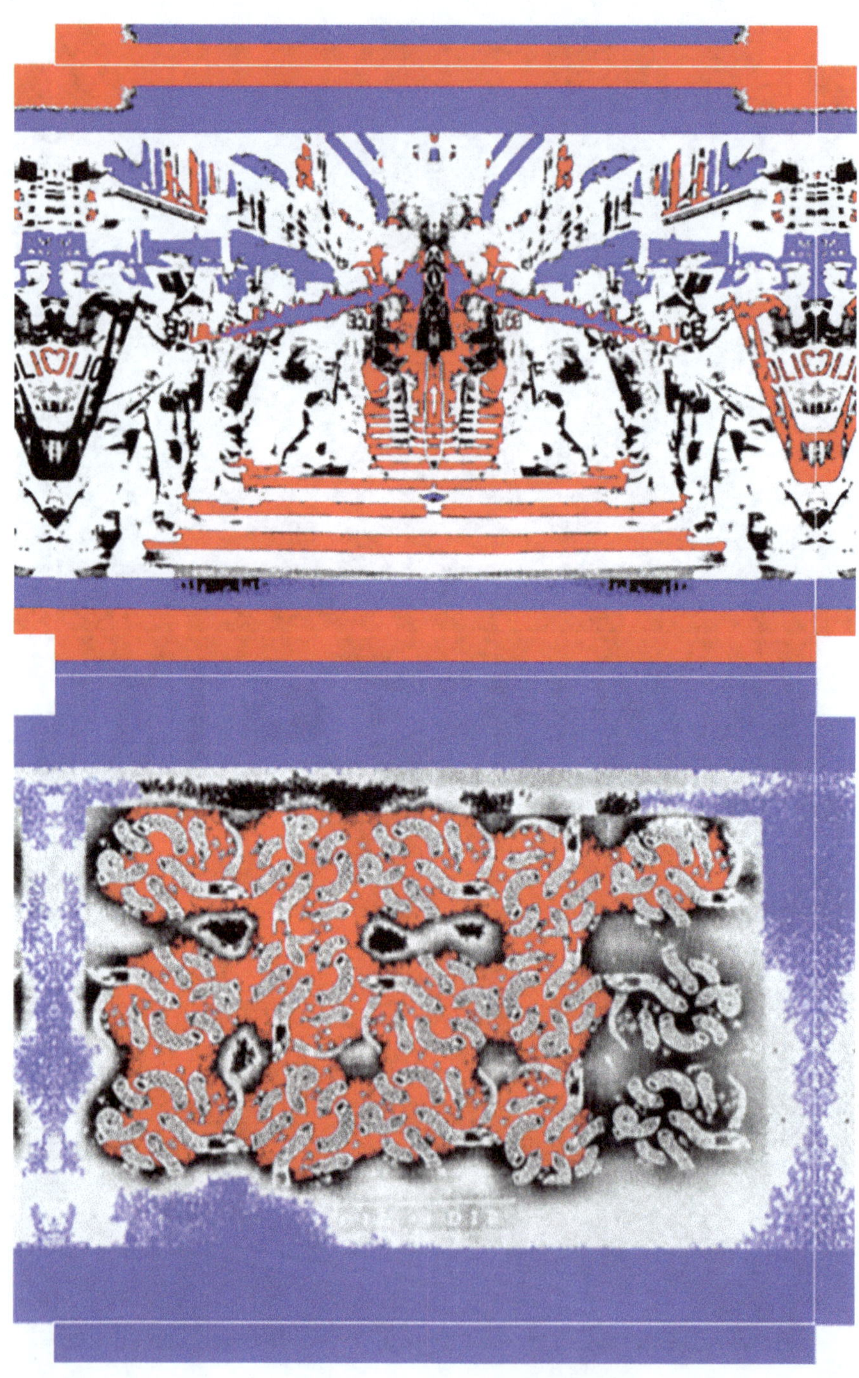

Commencement Speech
Clichés of Political Babble Poem (Decompress)

Pull your bootstraps up. A rose by any other name—it's all for one. Do you want to swim with the sharks? I'm all ears; then hop in the tank. You're fired. Don't get all bent out of shape; you may need to wrestle with the lions, tigers, and bears. Oh my, we got to run like the wind while running with the bulls. Really? Like flattery will get you nowhere. First we need to beat the street. Lately, there has been a brain drain. We need to do a brain dump. Gag me with a silver spoon. We cannot give any of them a clean bill of health. They have blood on their hands. We got an ace up our sleeve. The ball is in your court; you are the next generation. Around the horn we know it was a bad call. Having twenty-twenty vision and hindsight, do we wait until the bottom falls out? Refs call foul. Do we cry over spilled milk? Baby got back, and I want my baby back, baby back. Instead of being all over the map, do we face our fears? We need to do an about-face. Let all share in building that better mousetrap. The world will beat a path to your door. Grand opening, grand closing. There is no bait and switch, no rhyme or reason. The buck stops here. We know it may all bottom out. Your faith is being tested, but be resilient.

Freedom has its cost, and the price is right. You can't put freedom on layaway. We all know it was a bad call in the first place. But take the pledge: "We will not continue to do things ass-backward or bend over backward." If you do, you are up the creek without a paddle. Stop getting struck through the heart. You're blaming fame. Stick in the mud sucks. Instead, try catching a falling knife. Risk nothing without the reward of lost. For the business at hand, we must keep it strictly business. Let's burn the midnight oil. Let the businesses change hands and create that cash cow. Remember, the streets are watching. All mine is under my magic pillow. Dangle a carrot in front of them. Diamonds are a girl's best friend. Don't get blinded by the light. See the complete picture. We know it's a dog-eat-dog world, out there. So you better clean your plate. Wash it down by drinking the Kool-Aid. Make sure when you ride, you are firing on all cylinders. Dance on the ceiling and be the eight-hundred-pound gorilla in the room. Bang on the walls until the cops come knocking. We not going to take it, because we don't need no education. I can see clearly now—tear down this wall. Keep that dead cat bounce going, for as long as you could, like a faint pulse. Make that hard stop and take a U-turn to success. Make three sharp rights and get to your destination. Same place, less time. Start right now, dream a world that has yet to arrive. Click your heels three times and take that ride, next stop Oz. Follow the yellow brick, until you fall down the rabbit hole. Ask if this is it—blue or red pill? Be hands-off, and hands-on at the same time. Be the success you want to be, strive for greatness. Get your foot in the door. Problems, we got no problems? I got ninety-nine problems, and you ain't one.

Get your arms around them. If they say no, go over their head. Get that hand-to-hand combat, hands-on experience you need. Be the success you want, with the attitude you need, to strive to get ahead. Get the results you want, or leave if you need, you can achieve if you believe. Click your heels three times and say Candyman or Beetlejuice three times. Take it all in as it all goes down. You can open any door. Don't wish upon a star—have a star wish all over you. Live life in a golden pool, it will pay the bills. Close early and often, but be the red eye fly-by-nights that fly on the wall. Go in gang-busters. Remember, it's business; it's never personal. Take no shorts, but remember there are small people, with even smaller minds. So stomp them out. Be the good soldier. Keep trying to stay in the black, even if they tell you that light is right. Dollar-bill green—keep a green thumb. If you are in the red, you are dead.

A house divided against itself cannot stand, so knock on a neighbor's door because it's a hard-knock life. Live by a Jedi's sword, die by Vader's swords, only to be reborn. Be legendary in mind. Keep your nose to the grindstone and you can knock the ball out of the park. Hell, you can knock the cover off the ball. Like a coiled spring, jump into action. Buy low, sell high. Shoot for the stars, if you fall you lay in heaven's arms, or just outside the gates of hell. It doesn't matter if you waited all day in line, only that you got in, and that if you were late, at least you showed up.

Money matters, so have money on your mind and your mind on what matters. Be hooked on phonics, not on the phonies. Clap on, clap off, so don't forget to clap back at all. Players love the game, and do not hate. Haters love to hate, but hate playing the games. So love-hate the games all the way to success. As some are making money hand over fist, we don't want anyone left at the altar. Laugh all the way to the bank. It's mission critical, that we walk in rhythm, so free your mind. Open the kimonos and let the world see what's inside. Choose to pick the low-hanging fruit, instead of pounding the table, hoping it falls from the tree to your plate. Eat off your own plate and not others. Always look the part and act accordingly. While in the crisis we don't want anyone to take a bath, instead we hoped they did earlier and will also take one for the team. Off with his head, but don't be so emotional. Et tu, green-eyed monster? I was told to beware, by the queen of hearts. Leave it up to beaver and lie low. Love is blind, deaf, and Dumbledore. Technically speaking, I believe the game is afoot. Send them into overtime, and on a wild-goose chase. Follow the leader. It's safe to say tomorrow is only promised to one. Our father, which is in heaven. Just when I got out, they pulled me back in. Let's talk shop. I need your undivided attention. Try to think outside the box. This is high level, at a thirty-thousand-foot level. We are not thinking about yesterday, but the promise of tomorrow. Let's wipe the slate clean and start a new day. If you scratch my back, then give me some scratch. I want you to up the ante. So we are clear, there is a mole and plant, but there will be no Trojan Horse. As you know, time is money, and money can buy a lot of time. Together let's build that better mousetrap, think outside of the box, and move onward, ever onward. Today is the dawn, and tomorrow is not promised. If you are willing to swim with the sharks, pull yourself up by your bootstraps, and put a little sweat equity into it, and you will succeed! Can we talk shop? Let's sweeten the pot and pour out the Kool-Aid? Oh yeah! There are no sellouts, only sold-out concerts. If it's survival of the fittest. Remember, welfare feeds the hungry, corporate welfare greed fattens the arteries of the greedy. Let's all toast, but I'd be remised if I didn't remind you hoping they choke on wealth is not a good strategy. Strive, don't just try to occupy, because it's tea-party time, so party like it's 1999.

Let's not think what he's smoking and wish he'd choke on it. This thing of ours. Let's go out and get some and pass it around to fiends of ours. Let the good times roll, and dynamite, damn. Those were the days, moving on. Different strokes for same broke. While the getting is good, let's go get it. When the going gets tough, give up. Never do things, ass or cash backward. Unless you like getting the short end of the stick. Let's paint the town pink, and beat that cash cow, black and blue. Until the fat lady sings and scratch your back. I scratch yours with trickle-down economics. The same as trickle-down golden parachute. Remember, it's the economy stupid. So more pork sausages, Mom, please. Throwing cash into the wind and hoping it sticks is not a good savings plan. Be the bait and switch you need so you never wind up on Americas most wanted. If we live by the sword, then we have to deal with it. So spike the Kool-Aid. Don't think outside the box, put everyone inside one. Preferably one without windows, so they don't see it coming. When you're wealthy, the buck stops and stays here. Money comes in but doesn't go out. Remember the changing of guard and the pecking order can be different people, but the same uniform. So burn the midnight oil, and then make them pay for it. Another day, another dollar. Remember the Alamo, and the difference between an attaboy on the back and a condescending slap on the ass. Never do an attagirl. You're going number two instead of thinking of number one. You should have held your card instead of asking for a hit. They are not babes in the woods. You can catch a two-by-four to the jaw and wallet. He should have zigged, but you zagged, so zip it. The ball is in your court. At the drop of a hat, the crack of dawn, and as luck would have it. You could be the father. So give an arm and a leg—all bets are off. So cash in your chips—don't get caught with your pants down. Cowboy up, never cowgirl down. Be as crazy as a fox, cream of the crop. Life is a crapshoot. Good riddance and forget about it! Let's table this. What's on your mind? Under the weather. Spill the beans. Are you behind the eight ball, or long in the tooth with something to prove? Make it to first base? Don't be such a wet blanket. Do you have a green thumb or are you blue in the face? Shoot the breeze—it's a breeze. Scoot over. This is up my alley.

Class is in session. Put a sock on it before you get socked in it. Straight to the moon. Knock, knock; break a leg on a bridge to nowhere. Working the graveyard shift. What a lovely day. It's not rocket science, so put lipstick on a pig. It's a piece of cake, so have your cake and eat it too. Get yours, but don't be late to the party. So be a man with a plan. I'm not a big fan of Monday-morning quarterbacks.

COMING SOON

VOLUME II

CONCRETE

THE LEGACY

PLANTATION

CREATIVE ART & POETRY